PREY

Katy Mann

Blue Iris Books

PASADENA, CALIFORNIA

Kay Mann / Blue Iris Books
Pasadena, California
www.KatyMann.com

Publisher's Note: This is a work of fiction. Names, characters, places, and incidents are a product of the author's imagination. Locales and public names are sometimes used for atmospheric purposes. Any resemblance to actual people, living or dead, or to businesses, companies, events, institutions, or locales is completely coincidental.

Book Layout ©2013 BookDesignTemplates.com

Cover by Graphicz X Designs (http://graphiczxdesigns.zenfolio.com)

Blue Iris Books/ Katy Mann -- 1st ed.
ISBN 978-1-941646-00-7

Acknowledgements

To the many people who helped and encouraged me.

Special thanks to my beta reader, Jessica McKenna; my editor, Jennifer Silva Redmond; and to my mother, Jeanette Mann, without whom this book would not have been finished.

And special thanks to Rickie Bansbach, GeezerWench, Charletha Tatum, Sharon Laubach, and to my friends who kept asking if the book was on Amazon yet.

CHAPTER ONE

Seeing

The stranger was leaning casually against the front of the building. I almost missed seeing him as I was running late for work. When he caught my eye I paused, drawn to his long, lean figure. He wore a tan overcoat and a fedora pulled low, so I couldn't see his face. I shivered and gasped as intense fear flooded through me.

His head snapped in my direction, and a smile flitted across his face as if he heard me from across the street. He wore sunglasses, so I couldn't see his eyes. What I could see was a strong jaw and a classically handsome face, framed by shoulder-length brown hair.

The sound of a diesel engine caught my attention. I turned to see a bus drive away, and when I looked back, he was gone.

That frightened me more than anything else. He had been standing near the middle of the historic Monadnock Building, which covered an entire block. He couldn't possibly have gone inside or around a corner during the brief instant I was distracted, yet he had completely disappeared.

This was downtown Chicago, at 8:00 a.m. on a June morning. People swarmed around me on their way to work. I stood frozen, feeling the flow of people passing me, trying to make sense of my fear. Instead of going into my office, I walked in the opposite direction. I called my boss, Millicent, from a coffee shop two blocks away and told her I wasn't coming in. I forgot to say I was sick—in fact, I didn't give her any reason at all.

The line went silent for a few seconds, and then she asked, "Christa, what happened?"

What was I supposed to tell her? Some man leaning up against a wall scared me too much to show up for work? As I turned over my thoughts, seeking words to justify my behavior, she broke the silence, saying, "I hear people talking around you. Where are you? I'll come to you."

"Rosie's Treats. I'm sorry."

"Don't be," she said firmly. "It's important to trust your instincts."

CHAPTER TWO

Taking Shelter

The small coffee shop was bustling with early morning commuters, which was reassuring. Our law firm ordered coffee and refreshments from the shop for client meetings. I had been to it several times to pick up orders, and I liked its warm interior. There was a mural of a rose garden on the walls, which the owner told me had been painted from photos of her family's house in Indiana. It reminded me of the roses in front of my grandparents' house in Michigan. I ordered hot tea from the friendly owner and found a seat at a corner booth where I sat and waited for Millicent.

A short while later, her familiar figure stood in the doorway. Tall and elegantly dressed in a tailored suit, her graying hair pulled back in a small ponytail, she presented a striking figure. She lingered only a second in the doorway before spotting me; an artistic gold earring caught the light as she turned her head. Making her way across the crowded room to my table, she sat down across from me.

Now that she was there, looking at me with her piercing eyes, I felt like a fool for my reaction a few minutes earlier. I started to make apologies, but she waved them away.

"Tell me what happened."

"I just feel stupid," I replied, ducking my head in embarrassment.

"No," she said. "Follow your instincts. The firm often handles cases against unsavory clients."

"I saw a man," I said. "One minute he was there, the next he wasn't." The episode still didn't make sense to me. I wasn't a nervous, skittish person.

She leaned across the table and gave my hand a reassuring pat. "What did he look like?"

"Tall. Brown hair. He was wearing a hat and sunglasses, but he had a strong jaw and an attractive face. His hair was brown and shoulder length. And he wore a tan overcoat. That's all I can remember. Except that I was overwhelmed by fear. He seemed to sense it even though I was across the street."

I stared at my lap when I was done, hating to sound so weak. The image I wanted to project was one of efficiency. I looked back up and met her eyes.

Millicent leaned back in the booth, hands folded on the table. I thought I saw fear flit across her face, but she quickly smoothed it into her usual calm expression. She waited a minute as she often did when collecting her thoughts, then pulled out her phone and sent a text. After waiting a moment for the reply, she put her phone in her blazer pocket.

"I texted one of our investigators," she told me, "and I gave him the description you gave me. Once outside, he'll send me a message and then follow us back to the office. He's a professional, so we won't see him, but if someone is outside, I'm sure Mike will see him. Especially since he's wearing a hat and sunglasses at this hour of the morning."

She smiled and turned to our favorite topic, Paris.

She told me about her own trip to France five years earlier. Our conversations were usually about my dream of going to Paris and rarely about her own travels. It was nice to listen to her though I noticed she was watching me intently.

When she received a text, we walked back to the Monadnock Building. In the lobby we bypassed the old elevators and climbed the two flights of marble stairs to the third floor where the law firm Gupta, Berrywhite, Snow, LLC was located. I loved this building. It made me determined to land the position when I came for the interview. Others complained about the ancient elevators and long, echoing halls, but those were the very things that I loved. I would pause in the hallways, close my eyes, and imagine the people who had been here in the decades before I was born roaming the halls—tipping their hats to one another, working on the projects and contracts that shaped the present. The past was a refuge to me, safe and secure.

Gupta, Berrywhite, Snow, LLC was a small firm. A large reception desk dominated the entry room of the suite, and the partners' offices were behind that desk. To the left were the conference rooms and to the right of the receptionist's desk was the firm's law library.

We went into Millicent's office, and I sat down in one of the leather chairs while she took a call from a client. I looked around the familiar walls, focusing on the framed photographs. My eyes settled on a black and white photo of a large, elegant Rococo building on the edge of a canal. The photo was labeled "the Doge's Palace" in Millicent's fine handwriting on the lower right corner of the mat. Several boats, both gondolas and modern motorboats, were in front of the building. I noticed that their diminutive size helped give scale to the palace.

Her keen eyes watched me while she scribbled notes about the call and logged it onto her computer.

"That's the Doge's Palace in Venice," she said when she finished typing. "I stayed in Venice for a few weeks between college and law school. I took that shot early one morning from one of the taxi boats. It is very beautiful, yet in the Renaissance, it was the site of midnight trials and summary executions. I keep it in front of me as a reminder of how the beauty of a structure that is supposed to represent justice can hide the terror of the politics inside. I've always felt it my calling to represent those who cannot, for whatever reason, navigate the judicial system."

I momentarily lost myself imagining the dark world the Venetian palace represented. I loved populating scenes based on old photos, imagining those other lives and times.

I was pulled back from my reverie when she said in a formal tone, "For the rest of the week, I need you to do some research at a law library near the Evanston campus of Northwestern, on the north shore. It's a closed, private facility, but I'll make the arrangements for you to have access. Call me for your assignment when you get there each morning. Can you finish your work on the Converse case today?"

I told her that I could. She nodded, and as she picked up her phone, I left her office and went to my cubicle. That was the end of the morning's excitement over the stranger, and I was relieved to get to work.

I spent the rest of the day doing my usual paralegal work for Millicent, including filing forms and drafting documents. Routine paperwork was good. Organizing the present and creating schedules for the future, keeping it manageable was something I did. It kept the starkness of the future's empty, unknowable space at bay. I ate lunch with one of the other law clerks, Georgina, and she filled me in on her escapades at a club the night before. By the end of the work day, the morning's terror seemed nothing more than a strange moment.

Outside on the street, the fear returned. I felt like someone just out of sight was following me. Once on the bus, I scanned the sidewalk. Though I didn't see anyone, I couldn't shake the feeling of being watched.

When I got to my stop in the Near North, I didn't go directly to my apartment. I walked the tree-lined streets to several nearby stores, including my neighborhood grocery store and dry cleaners, ducking into each one for a few minutes. I looked out the doors before leaving but didn't see anyone outside lingering, waiting for me. Chicago is a city that walks, and the sidewalks were full of pedestrians. Finally, I felt it was safe enough to head home.

CHAPTER THREE

The Job

M y cat Boo was waiting for me when I opened my apartment door, rubbing against my leg. I picked him up, burying my face in his fur, letting his purr relax me. I'd grabbed the mail on my way up and sorted out my few letters from the junk mail my friend had received. Today I had a postcard from her from Finland. I sighed. Some people had that kind of money. They could travel where they wanted while the rest of us felt lucky to sublet their empty condo.

The message light on the phone was flashing, so I set Boo down and pushed the button. I am old-fashioned and prefer using a landline. I keep my cell phone only for emergencies and turn it off when I am at work or in class. Strike that. I keep it turned off most of the time. The first message was from my mother. "Darling, we've been invited by the Dovers to go out on Lake Michigan with them over the 4th of July weekend," her voice began. "It's been a while since we've seen them. Should I tell them we'll both come?"

I had to smile. Janice Dover had a son my age named Trevor. Good looking and way out of my league though neither of our mothers seemed to know that. I think they married us off when we were three years old. Trevor had dutifully squired me to various political functions my mother invited us to throughout the years. He made a dashing figure in a tuxedo and, unlike me, was very good at the easy banter of a cocktail party or reception. He also knew how to handle a sailboat. Spending the weekend sailing sounded fun.

I called her back, and when I got her voicemail, left a message. "Tag, you're it. Of course I want to go sailing over the holiday. See you Thursday."

The next message from Millicent startled me. "Just wanted to make sure you got home all right. Call me if you see anyone suspicious in your neighborhood or anywhere else. I can get Mike to give you a ride to Evanston tomorrow morning if you would like."

After listening to the message twice, I deleted it. I was lucky to have someone who took my fears seriously.

I made a cup of tea and collapsed into one of the chairs at my dining room table. Boo jumped on my lap, and I petted him absently.

The job I had with the law firm was a summer internship. My college guidance counselor had set me up with the interview, advising me that this was considered an ideal position for pre-law students. I should dress appropriately, she stressed, and sound certain that I wanted to be a lawyer when interviewed.

She had looked pointedly at my scruffy loafers, which I pulled back under my chair.

I thanked her, took the paperwork, and went back to the library. In addition to studying for finals, I also did a little research on the firm. Founded just a few years ago, they hadn't been involved in any famous cases, but there were news articles about them. Cases won, cases lost. No splashy clients—they represented individuals against corporations and public institutions like hospitals.

On the appointed day, I polished my one pair of pumps, opened a new package of stockings, and put on my black wool skirt paired with a white sweater. I pulled my hair back into a bun and took the bus to the address in downtown Chicago, to the historic Monadnock Building. Squaring my shoulders, I went in and told the receptionist I was there for a meeting with one of the partners.

During the interview, I foolishly told my interviewer, Millicent Berrywhite, the truth. That I was a history major and wasn't sure whether I wanted to be a lawyer, but I did want to be a researcher and thought this internship would help develop my skills.

To my surprise, she hired me anyway.

We spoke a little about her firm and its clients. It was a new company, formed by Millicent and a few of her law school friends. Upon graduation they had pooled their money and formed their own law firm with the goal of representing the "little people," who might not otherwise be able to afford justice.

She admitted that this occasionally meant going up against unsavory litigants—she'd even bumped heads with the Mafia a few times. She couldn't give me details, but it sounded exciting to a mousy girl from the suburbs.

Even though my mother was a Field Representative for the 28th Ward Alderwoman, I hadn't had much experience with crime. We had moved to Chicago after my father's death when I was ten. Before that, we had lived in Oak Park, close to my father's small architectural firm. The business, specializing in historic reconstruction, had closed when he died and my mother moved into the city to be closer to her parents.

As the weeks passed, Millicent became friendlier, and we sometimes ate our lunch together. On one of those occasions, I told her of my dream to go to Paris after graduation.

She smiled and said that anything was possible. Why shouldn't I go? was her attitude. She encouraged me to plan for it and to study the city and its history. She told me I shouldn't expect the people to be terribly different than they were here, and in her experience, not everyone was good.

I guessed that today I had run into one of those "unsavory" clients and hoped I wasn't in any real danger.

CHAPTER FOUR

Missing

My new research location was a dusty old library near Northwestern's Evanston campus. The bus stopped close to the campus, and since I was early, I walked onto the quad to get a view of Lake Michigan. I spent a few minutes by the lake, feeling the cool breeze on my face, listening to the sound of the water and watching the birds wheeling overhead. Scenes like this were one of the reasons that I'd wanted my own apartment. I loved being able to walk to Lake Michigan at any time and to watch how it changed over the seasons. The lake was never silent. Even now, alone on the rocks, the sound of the waves breaking below me and the ever-present gulls above took me out of my own life. These rocks, waves, and gulls would be present no matter who stood watching.

When the appointed time came, I made my way to a nondescript, gray brick building. Once properly signed in, a man who could have been cast as the Crypt Keeper showed me the cavernous reading room. Clearly, my presence was a novelty in this normally silent space. He climbed up ladders and brought down the books and journals I requested, hovering over me while I read. I knew he was being helpful, but I was getting spooked.

I couldn't shake the feeling of someone else in the library with us. Someone I couldn't see, just on the other side of the stacks. My Crypt Keeper helper never seemed to notice anything, but I heard rustlings and small sounds that ceased as soon as I looked up.

I slogged through the material making notes on my laptop while sitting at one of the long wooden tables dotted with bankers lamps in the quiet room. I wanted to finish as soon as possible and get back downtown where I didn't have to deal with eerie rustlings while I worked.

At the end of the afternoon I phoned Millicent with my results, e-mailed my research notes, and got my next assignment. By the end of the second day, I hoped she would tell me to come back to her office. But she didn't. With each of my reports, I was opening up a new line of investigation, so she needed me to look further into the journal references I had located.

Which was what I was supposed to be doing, right? Reminding myself that I was improving my research skills, which might lead to a better reference from her, I kept up my pace and asked the Crypt Keeper for more journals.

Each night I took the bus home, checked my mail, and fed Boo. The cat was my one constant companion. My few friends had mostly gone home for the summer. We stayed in touch by Facebook and e-mail, but Boo was the one who was there for me when I needed to talk. My only close friend, Stacey, was from high school. Since I didn't live in the dorms, it had been harder to make friends in college. Being able to sublet the condo had been an enormous step for me, as it meant not just moving out of the family home but also living alone.

I had found Boo as a kitten, hiding behind a dumpster by a grocery store. Mom wanted to take him to a shelter, but I'd prevailed on my father to let me keep him. My father could never tell me no.

I used to be an assertive, outgoing girl. The older sister, the first one to try something new. That changed the day my father had his heart attack. We were driving to Chicago, just the two of us in the SUV. He grabbed at his arm and fought to stay alert while he wove the car across three lanes of traffic onto the shoulder. When we hit the guard rail, the airbags inflated. Most of what happened after was a blur. I remember people were outside the car, getting us out. They wouldn't let me see him as they put him in the ambulance. They let me ride in the police car to the hospital where my grandfather waited with me until my mother came.

I gasped. How quickly the terrifying memory slipped into my present. I clutched the table, focusing on the hallway mirror in front of me. I reached down and felt for Boo. "If only you had been with me today," I told him. "I probably could have gotten to the bottom of the mystery. Right?"

Boo rubbed against my leg and purred before sitting down to clean his front paws. I picked him up and stared at our reflection in the mirror. His silky black coat stood in stark contrast to my blonde hair. His fur glistened with health. My short, lifeless blonde hair hung on either side of my head. Examining myself critically, I sighed.

"I'm getting too thin," I told Boo. I seldom felt like eating in the heat, and from the look of the bags under my eyes, I was getting anemic again. Before seeing my mother I would need to lather on make-up. During lunch I could take walks to get some color on my face.

I decided to be more careful with my diet and made a healthy lunch to take to the law library in the morning. While making dinner, I looked out the window and checked the passersby on the sidewalk. I didn't see anyone loitering. I shook my head, disgusted with myself. Why would there be anyone? Who would be interested in me?

The next day when I called in, Millicent didn't answer. One of the other partners from the firm, Jeremy Gupta, did.

"Miss Swenson, I'm glad you called. It's odd, but Ms. Berrywhite isn't here yet. She has always been the first one in. I'm not used to having to open the office myself."

Despite my worry, I smiled to myself, picturing the brilliant, if somewhat nervous, man attempting something as practical as unlocking the office suite.

"Do you know anything about her calendar?" he continued.

"I don't," I said. "But I know that she called one of the firm's investigators a few mornings ago."

He paused and then continued. "Thank you for that information. Usually she tells me when she calls an investigator. I'll contact him to see if he knows anything. Maybe she's interviewing a client this morning. Come back downtown, and we'll find something for you to do."

Back in the Monadnock Building, I spent the day in a room with musty old boxes, reviewing medical records for a list of scary-sounding medical terms while worrying about Millicent. In one file, I saw the name Moltadano written and underlined in the margin of a deposition in her familiar handwriting. Moltadano. The name sounded Italian and ancient as if there might be a fascinating history behind it. I could picture intrigues in the Medici court associated with bearers of this name. I rolled it over on my tongue, pulled the folder out and looked through it. It was a suspicious death case, and the coroner had not been able to make a final determination of the cause of death. It was the only case I found that she had worked on. I carefully put the folder back in the box and continued reviewing the files as requested.

A few days passed this way. The only change was that someone rolled in a comfortable chair for me. I thought it must have been my friend Georgina, but the receptionist whispered that it was Mr. Gupta.

Walking to my bus stop each afternoon, I couldn't shake the feeling of being watched though I never saw anyone. I kept hoping to see Millicent coming around the corner, carrying her Starbucks, with some explanation for her absence.

The following Monday morning when I came in, I could sense nervousness vibrating through the office suite.

The receptionist, usually so friendly, greeted me in a cool tone. "Good morning, Christa. Mr. Gupta is waiting for you in Ms. Berrywhite's office." One of the law clerks standing by her desk was staring at me, then dropped her eyes when I looked her way.

I walked past the reception desk to the familiar suite. Pausing before the door, I knocked. Mr. Gupta opened the door and gestured for me to come inside. As I entered, I saw two police officers. The men stood as I entered and remained standing after I took the chair across from Mr. Gupta. The silence in the room unnerved me, and I fidgeted as I waited for someone to speak. I felt I was being assessed.

"Millicent still hasn't come in," Mr. Gupta said, unable to hide his concern for his friend and partner. "These officers have just come from her condo. It doesn't appear she's been there either. Looking through her notes in her desk, I found an envelope entitled 'In the Event I Go Missing'."

I felt all eyes on me as I looked at the envelope in his hand. I shivered. "She expected this?"

"I don't know. She never expressed any concerns about her safety to me, and I would like to think that she would have. But what is interesting about this package is what was inside." He held up the large manila envelope. "Just a blank piece of paper and this."

He pulled out a smaller envelope. "It contains an airline ticket and cash inside an envelope with your name, Christa Swenson, on it."

He leaned across the desk and handed it to me.

I opened it with shaking hands, as both he and the officers watched. I couldn't suppress my gasp of surprise. It held a ticket to Paris in my name, along with a small stack of fifty dollar bills and a blue Post-It note on the face of the ticket. Millicent had written a single word in her familiar, neat handwriting: "Go."

CHAPTER FIVE

The Missing Millicent

I stayed at the law firm and completed the remainder of my two-month internship, still hoping, as the days dragged on, that Millicent would return safely.

She never did.

A week after her disappearance, I had conversations with both the investigator, a man introduced only as Mike, and Jeremy Gupta.

Mike went over the incidents of that June morning with me several times.

The first time, we met with the police officers and Mr. Gupta present.

"Tell me again about that morning, Christa," Mike said. "What were you doing?"

"I was on my way to work," I stated. "As I approached the office, this man caught my eye. He was leaning against the building."

"Go on," Mike said. "What did he look like?"

"Tall. Brown hair to his shoulders. He wore a fedora and sunglasses."

"Did you get a look at his face?"

"It seemed to me he was handsome. He had a large mouth, strong jaw."

"Had you ever seen him before?" asked one of the police officers.

"No," I answered.

"Have you seen him since?" the officer asked.

"No, and I've been looking," I replied.

Mike stared at the police officer who had spoken, waiting.

"Continue, I just wanted to get those facts," the officer replied.

"So he didn't say anything to you?" Mike asked.

"I only saw him from across the street. But he looked right at me, looked me full in the face," I said, shivering involuntarily at the memory.

There was a short silence.

"You were afraid?" Mike asked gently.

"Yes. That's what was strange."

"Why? Did he have his hands in his pockets? Did he look dangerous?"

"No, none of those things. He just…I don't know. He scared me. It seemed as if he knew it because he looked straight at me."

The detective and the two men exchanged glances while the police officers shuffled their papers.

"Thank you, Miss Swenson. If you think of anything else, please let us know," Mike said as he concluded the interview.

Jeremy, on the other hand, was more interested in why Millicent left me the money and ticket to go to Europe. He didn't seem to have any issues with the fact that she did; he just wanted to get a better understanding of why. I couldn't answer him, other than to tell him she knew I had wanted to go, just as she knew I couldn't afford to go.

When I told him that, he smiled. "That's why she wanted to send you. She was a hard worker, but she believed in dreams. In the short time I've known you, I've noticed that you seem totally focused on the reality in front of you. But that's not everything in life. There is so much more, and you need to make time for dreams as well."

On the 4th of July weekend, I went sailing with Trevor. We talked about many things including his recent engagement to a girl he had met at Northwestern. She was pre-med with plans to be a surgeon. So much for our mothers' plans for us.

July passed quickly. I saw my high school-aged brother and sister several times. Simon and Simone were in summer camp together enjoying their outdoor adventures of camping and hiking. It sounded great to me except for wearing hiking boots, carrying a back-pack, and sleeping in a tent. I preferred sleeping in beds and taking the train to my destinations. I was happy at the twins' easy enjoyment of life. They had been young when our father died and barely remembered him. I had been in the car with him on the freeway when he had the heart attack, so I would never forget. One moment he was there; the next he wasn't. My world had been split in two. Before that day, the future was a source of curiosity and hope. After the car crash, I realized the world could be split into the past and present in seconds.

The feeling of being followed seemed to evaporate about a week after Millicent disappeared. During the daytime anyway. At night, though, my dreams were haunted by the memories and fear experienced the day I saw the stranger.

The sight of the money in the envelope both shocked and elated me. After my father died, money was tight. My mother raised my brother, sister, and me alone. I was in college on full scholarship and only able to afford the apartment because a friend sublet it to me during her year of study abroad. I split Millicent's cash gift in half, deciding to use half for my final school year and the other half for traveling.

Millicent and her generous gift had given me wings, and I chose to fly. No more just dreaming of the City of Lights. I wanted to ask my friend Stacy to go with me, but she had just gotten married in May, so I decided to go solo. It would give me a chance to be adventurous, I told myself. I could spend my time visiting historical sites, browsing bookstores, or exploring. Doing whatever I wanted, whenever I wanted to. Plus, as my practical side reminded me, there was time for this trip before the next semester began, so I made my arrangements. When the eight-week summer internship ended in August, I would go to Paris.

That I had been given such a generous gift had the police interested in me, but in the end they agreed to let me travel abroad, providing I advised them of where I was staying. The fact that my mother worked for an Alderwoman probably helped.

My mother would take care of Boo while I was gone, and I left my plants in the care of a friendly neighbor across the hall. Mom drove me to the airport the day I was to depart on my adventure. As I opened the door to get into her car, I glanced up and saw Boo looking down from his window perch. His green eyes glowed as they reflected the light from a street lamp, and I smiled and waved, watching his mouth form a sound I couldn't hear.

CHAPTER SIX

The Trip

I arrived in Paris the first week of August.

My hotel was a charming place a few blocks from the Paris Opera. It was an older hotel, a tall narrow building that blended in with the other businesses on the street. My tiny room was clean, with a thick blue and white bedspread on a bed that took up most of the space. The bathroom was small as well—the barest necessities, all in white porcelain. They served croissants and coffee in the small lobby for breakfast, so I ate there each morning, listening to the birds in a large birdcage sing. The only other guests were two French-Canadian couples who I exchanged polite "Good-mornings" with every day.

I quickly discovered that Paris closes in August. The Parisians go on holiday—to Spain, Greece, or wherever it is that those in the know go. I walked the city with my guidebook, taking in the sights and snapping photos.

The city center, unlike Chicago, was not filled with skyscrapers. Most of the buildings at the city center were six stories high, and only a single sleek, modern building towered over the graceful, older ones. A number of high-rise apartment buildings lined the far-off perimeter of the city.

Though the Metro stations with their iconic wrought-iron entrances and signs were easy to find, I preferred to walk. There was so much to see that I felt any time spent below the streets meant missing something above ground.

I enjoyed walking the city, watching the people pass me on the sidewalks, coming across cafes with chairs and tables placed strategically in front. I wanted to see it all, and I was sure two weeks would not be long enough.

While at the Louvre, I was struck by the magnificent statue of the Winged Victory, enthroned at the top of a grand staircase. I spent a long time standing in front of the headless, armless woman, the wings on her back unfurled, unable to tear myself away. According to a British guide who had paused in front of the statue with her group as she lectured in her clipped voice, the piece was notable for showing a pose hovering between motion and stillness as a wind blew across her marble garment.

All I could think about was the missing Millicent. Somehow this stone figure of a strong, beautiful woman bereft of her head and arms reminded me of her. Who or what had she fought against, and had she lost that struggle?

Millicent stayed foremost in my thoughts though I tried to lose myself in the accumulated beauty and culture of this fabled city.

In addition to the museums, I visited the bookstalls lining the Seine and the bookstores scattered nearby. None of the stores seemed to have the right feel. One of the things I liked best about bookstores was skimming through books. Here, I would walk in and be stopped by one or two saleswomen and not allowed to handle the books. They clearly didn't want customers to touch the merchandise, so I left.

While strolling in the Latin Quarter, a small bookstore caught my eye. A charming place, with an intricately detailed, wrought-iron bannister that guided the passerby three steps down from the street to the entrance.

CHAPTER SEVEN

The Bookstore

I opened the door and fell in love with the place. It felt old inside like there had been a long-time appreciation of books. There were more books than anyone could sell; sales clearly weren't the point. There were texts of quality and worth, works that would appeal to a collector, not just stacks of best sellers and coffee-table books on display tables.

The proprietor was an older man, who didn't seem bothered by the fact that I was an American. After guessing that I wanted to browse, he sat down at his antique desk and rustled a few papers while typing on his computer. I had a feeling it was just for show, and this was his way of letting me browse in peace though he kept a solicitous watch over me as all the shopkeepers did.

As I looked through the tall wooden bookshelves that lined the store, for some reason the name I saw in the file back in Chicago, Moltadano, popped back into my head. Out of curiosity, I decided to look for anything on family names. The name sounded Italian, so I asked the proprietor for the location of Italian studies.

He raised an eyebrow. "A beautiful girl in my beautiful city, and you are asking about an Italian? Should I be jealous?"

I laughed. "It's just information about a family. I ran across the name once, and it stuck with me. The name was Moltadano. Have you heard of them?"

"Ah, you should be looking in France, then, ma petite. The Moltadano family left Italy centuries ago. They lived here for a while and then vanished. I've heard it said that they maintain a residence in Rouen. A very old family, very...reticent. They like their privacy. Are your studies in mythology? You might look there."

I was thinking he was going to direct me to the crime section. But mythology? I don't think gangsters are a myth.

He pulled down a book with an aged leather binding. I loved the rich, red cover and black binding before he even opened it.

"You like books," he said. "I can see that. Even the cover has you interested?"

"Yes," I answered with a smile. "I'm a bookworm."

"Bookworm?" He looked puzzled.

"That's what they call girls like me back home."

"Here, we call girls like you 'belle,'" he said smoothly.

I laughed. "My name is Christa, actually."

He raised an eyebrow, then pulled down a book. "Here is a book on the city of Rouen. It is not far, so you could visit it."

I opened the volume, turning the pages gently, sensing the owner watching me. When I glanced up, I saw a slight smile on his face.

"You appreciate books, I can see from the care you use. So many today they just rip through them or even read them on a computer."

I dropped my eyes as I thought about the Kindle app on my laptop.

"But you, you love books. That is good. The young must read," he said, more to himself than to me. He reached up to realign a book spine that was not perfectly in line with the rest.

A phone rang, and he bowed before going to answer it.

As I watched him walk to the front of the store, my eye was caught by something on a shelf above his head. I pulled the library ladder over and found another book, out of reach. It appeared quite old, the leather expensive and embossed with a circle containing a flying wedge inside, an image that looked like bird wings.

When the bookseller came around the corner, he froze at the sight of what was in my hands. The smile left his face, and he took the book from me, muttering that he had not meant for it to be on the shelf. He seemed to retreat deep inside of himself, closing up and hiding something painful, then he recovered and smiled again. Apologizing profusely, saying, "Another customer, she called inquiring after the title just this morning. I had not yet pulled it for her. I am sorry that you found it."

Puzzled, I thanked him and looked around some more, wondering what harm could come from reading a book.

As if in answer, the door chime rang, and the owner started toward the front of the store. He paused as he looked at the new customer who was hidden from my sight by the bookcase. Setting the book down on an open space in a shelf out of the newcomer's view, he finally said, "Bonjour, Monsieur." His voice shook slightly as he spoke.

CHAPTER EIGHT

The Legend

His hand hidden behind the bookshelves, the bookseller silently pointed me to the back door before stepping forward to greet his customer.

I grabbed the forbidden book from the shelf and flipped it over to look for a price tag. There wasn't one, so I placed twenty euros on a nearby table, hoping that would be enough, and slipped out the door he had pointed to.

Leaving the store, my heart beat wildly at the strange ending to what should have been a simple shopping trip.

Though it felt foolish, I practically ran to the nearest Metro Station, attracting strange looks from passersby as I dashed through the crowds. I wanted to get to the safety of my hotel. In my room I kicked off my shoes and flopped down on the bed, anxious to see what mysteries this forbidden book might hide. I flipped through the pages of the travel book, disappointed to find that it was just an illustrated guide to cities and lore of the Italian countryside. I turned it over in my hands, wondering why the bookseller was so reluctant for me to have it. It appeared to be an ordinary, if beautifully illustrated, travel guide from the mid-nineteenth century.

Until, that is, I reached the middle. The book fell open to a passage that had obviously been consulted frequently, "The Legend of the Moltadano."

The chapter preface noted that the narrator was chronicling an interview with a local Italian man who had heard the story from his great-grandfather.

This region, the chapter began, had been plagued with vampires. Blood-sucking demons preyed mostly on the young, generally when they were away from their houses working in the fields. Their preferred victims appeared to be young women, especially servant girls, who went missing quite frequently.

The solution finally arrived when a stranger, Signore Moltadano from Southern Italy, appeared before the city council. He advised that for a fee he would rid the city of the demons. He wanted a piece of civic treasure, a ring from the city church's collection. The priests were opposed as the ring belonged to a local saint, Saint Maria. But the council persuaded the clergy that the safety of the living should override any concerns about honoring the past.

And who knew if the stranger would succeed?

The city council agreed to the stranger's price. If the city went for a year without an attack, they would give him the requested relic.

He bowed and vanished. A week later he returned with twelve bodies which he displayed in the town square for the council. Oddly, though they were dead, the bodies looked fresh. Signore Moltadano set fire to the corpses which became animated as they burned, writhing and screaming. Eventually they were reduced to ashes as smoke rose to the sky, and silence fell over the crowd.

The horrific ordeal terrified the townspeople. They broke their covenant with Signore Moltadano and even managed to have the Moltadano family banished from Italy.

I shivered.

In the margin of this chapter there was a handwritten note. A reader had asked, "No crosses, no stakes?"

The answer, written neatly beneath, read: "Not in the legends of the Moltadano. No, there are none. Paris is an old city. We have our gargoyles for protection, but are they enough?"

Just what I needed, I thought with a grimace. A new spooky story when I was already jumpy. I decided to return the book in the morning.

That night I dreamt of monsters and saints. The monsters fought the valiant clergy for both the living and the body of the saint while the city councilors stood by and debated. I woke sitting up in bed, sweating. As I looked out the window, struggling to stay awake long enough for the dream to dissipate, I saw a movement in the darkened streets below, so I pulled back slightly from the window and waited. A cat stalked through the gutter and pounced on something I couldn't see. I laughed. Just a cat. I crawled back into bed and went back to sleep.

The next morning, I retraced my steps back to the small bookshop. When I arrived, the shop sign was turned to "Fermee," closed.

I spent the rest of the day wandering Paris. I found a weird exhibit at the medieval museum, Cluny. In addition to the famed Lady and the Unicorn tapestries, the museum housed a collection of reliquaries, elaborate miniature chapels containing the bones of saints. Gruesome, I thought. It made me wonder if the saint's ring in the tale of Moltadano contained one of her bones or teeth. The thought made me shiver.

Walking its streets, I saw that Paris is not just a monument to the past. The present surrounded me, pressing in from all sides in the sounds of traffic and passersby. So I tried to focus on this vital, living world as well as on the art and history of the beautiful capital. The city had elegant apartment buildings, another intersection of past and present. Current residents in the stately buildings made Paris' streets graceful. Gazing up at the edifices from the sidewalk, I frequently saw cats looking back down at me. Some were Persians, clad in well-combed coats of gray, white, or black. Others were ordinary house cats. They reminded me of my cat Boo. Occasionally I saw a cat on the street, and I would reach for it, hoping to soothe my homesickness with a rub, but the cats were too quick for me to touch.

That night, I strolled along the Seine, my hand tracing the tops of the partitions separating the sidewalk from the dark river that passed below. I found a bench along the bridge, where I sat down and watched the water flowing by while listening to the soft rippling. The sound relaxed me, reminding me of nights spent by Lake Michigan, when I had closed my eyes and lost myself in the ebb and flow of the lake's tide. The sound tonight was similar. I dropped into my usual reverie, thinking of who might else have passed this way. Whispered exchanges between elegantly clad, clandestine lovers from the Belle Époque or intrigues plotted by the revolutionaries and counterrevolutionaries from the Reign of Terror. People meeting where there would be no eavesdropping, the passing Seine the only witness to their dreams.

I came back from my reveries into the present. I felt I was missing something, something that was in front of me.

I heard footsteps behind me, steps that echoed on the empty streets. When I turned and looked, I didn't see anyone. The streets were empty—I should return to my room. I got up and hurried back. Close to the Opera, there were people on the street, so I relaxed. Still I was glad to reach the safety of the hotel. The desk attendant wished me, "Bon soir, Mademoiselle," as I made my way to the elevator. Once in my room I locked the door and checked to see if my window was locked. That night, the night sound of the flowing river filled my dreams.

The following morning I went back to the bookstore. I wasn't surprised to see a policeman standing in front of the door.

I shivered, feeling oddly responsible. The policeman's presence confirmed my sense of foul play. Should I come forward, tell them what I knew?

If I did, what could I say? That I'd been in the shop, and the bookseller seemed afraid of a customer I never saw?

I had felt a presence, though, something that tingled the edge of my senses just as in Chicago.

I mingled in the crowd and picked up what I could. A chatty baker told me the bookstore owner had locked his shop as usual two nights ago but didn't open the next morning. As he hadn't told this neighbor of vacation plans, the man made inquiries and learned the bookseller never made it home. The police found his body inside his store.

I couldn't pick up any other details about what had happened. It seemed people stopped whispering when they saw me. I assumed this was because I was a foreigner eavesdropping on a neighborhood tragedy.

I got the feeling of being watched and looked around. A tall, handsome man with dark hair and sunglasses seemed to disappear into the crowd. The brief glimpse I had of him gave me chills. Was he real? He seemed to slip into the crowd with such ease as if the people weren't aware of him. They didn't know to be afraid of him.

I walked back toward the Seine and my hotel. Would it be better to go to a church? The Cathedral of Notre Dame was nearby. I went to the bridge and stood watching the water pass below. People passed me, and they didn't look terrified. A sightseeing boat slid under the bridge, a guide with a megaphone speaking in German to his passengers. I gripped the stone railing tightly and looked up. Overhead a few birds circled then flew gracefully to the other side of the river. I envied them their freedom to fly where they wished, living above this beautiful city. Standing on the ground below them, I felt terror-stricken and earthbound.

This was a vacation. I didn't have to stay here—I could always come back when I felt calmer. Maybe I just

needed some distance between myself and the local tragedy of the bookseller. Without returning to my hotel, I
went to the train station and bought a ticket for the next
train to Italy.

Once I was settled on board, I called my hotel and
explained that circumstances had required me to depart
unexpectedly and requested they ship my few belongings
back to Chicago.

I leaned back in the seat and looked out the window.
Opening the travel book again, I read about Venice.

CHAPTER NINE

Venice

After a ten-hour train ride, I arrived in Venice. I easily found the pension I'd contacted from the train and picked up a few articles of clothing from a small shop nearby.

When I arrived in my room, I washed my face then stared in the mirror at the haggard face that stared back. *You need to get a grip. You just fled a city without your luggage because you were afraid...of* what? Maybe the old man simply had a heart attack, and the people were gathered because he was a long-time neighbor. I took a deep breath, then another.

Finally, somewhat calmer, I went to the windows and looked out. The pension looked over a canal, and the boats tied along it gently bobbed on the water. The late afternoon sun lit the scene beautifully. This was Venice after all.

Early the next morning I was in the central plaza, St. Mark's Square. Shops were opening, and café owners were setting out tables and chairs. Waves of pigeons rose from the cobblestones and flew around me and around the square, their bodies lifting and moving as one. I watched them circling against the sky and noticed a winged figure atop the main building. It had to be St. Mark. Below him was an image of a winged lion holding a book open with one paw.

Looking through my guidebook, bought at the train station, I walked around the square. I didn't feel like entering any of the tiny shops. I needed to be in sunlight, to be part of a crowd. The people around me who were seated at tables, talking happily as they drank their coffee and ate pastries, gave me a reassuring feeling of normalcy.

Reaching the Doge's Palace, I decided to go in. This was the building whose image Mildred had chosen to adorn her office.

I wandered in awe through palatial splendor, imagining a world where people lived in such luxury. But all the while I felt someone was watching me. Stepping back out into the sun, I squared my shoulders, reminding myself that these were all public places, and I was safe.

I wanted to see the Bridge of Sighs, the famous span that condemned prisoners had to cross on their way to prison. Stepping into the narrow passageway of the covered bridge, I saw a shadowy figure standing at the other end. Deep inside I felt something dark lurking ahead. It was just like when I'd seen the stranger in Chicago and the man at the edge of the crowd outside of the bookseller's shop in Paris. I was terrified as if my own freedom were at stake.

I turned and ran back into the main building then out into the square. Once in the sunlight, my fears again dissipated, but I felt alone in the crowd. I didn't speak Italian, so the language barrier contributed to my fear.

The age of this city, which seemed so perilously close to sinking into the Adriatic, was dragging me under. At heart I felt something was wrong with me. I needed to go home.

CHAPTER TEN

Race to Milan

I checked out of my pension, but, refusing to give in to fear, I took the train to Milan. I found a seat on the crowded train, surrounded by the chatter of the other passengers. I closed my eyes for a few minutes, letting their voices envelop me as they spoke Italian and French. The comforting sounds and the bright, open views of the Tuscan countryside relaxed me, and I felt the fear slip further away with each mile between myself and Venice.

This was a vacation, and I was determined to enjoy it. I wouldn't get the feeling of terror and the sensation of being watched everywhere in Italy. When I got home, I would check with student health. See if there was a pill for paranoia. I snorted. Yeah, I was sure there was a pill for that. In the meantime surely I could forget my fears for a few hours.

The train pulled into Milan around noon. After carrying my travel bag to a small hotel under the blistering August sun, I decided to explore.

I picked up a few brochures and saw that Leonardo da Vinci's Last Supper was nearby, so I decided to see that first. Advance tickets were required to enter the monastery, but I lucked out and managed to buy a ticket from a scalper. I'm sure he didn't have any trouble picking out the American tourist as I leaned against a wall and looked forlornly across the street, purse on my shoulder and water bottle under my arm as I thumbed through my guidebook. I broke a number of laws buying a ticket from him, but this might be my only chance to see the famous work. I pulled out one of Millicent's fifty-dollar bills, and the scalper was happy.

The iconic image had been painted on the monastery's dining hall—it was considered a miracle it had survived the Allied bombings of World War II. Staring up at the scene that covered the wall during the fifteen minutes allotted to me, I saw that the faces of Christ's disciples showed anger and shock, emotions the familiar commercial images had softened. I studied each man in turn, looking at the range of emotions shown on their faces and in their body language. I was so engrossed another viewer bumped into me. I smiled and murmured a "no problem" to what I assumed was an apology as I couldn't understand what he said. My group was ushered out too soon, and I was back on the street, blinking in the sunlight.

Outside, I bought a postcard as a souvenir from one of the vendors lining the sidewalks. Shadows lengthened in the late afternoon, bringing relief from the August sun overhead.

After consulting my guidebook for the next must-see attraction, I headed to the famous Milan Cathedral only a short distance away. I arrived just before 4:00.

The cathedral was an ornate, imposing structure that occupied one side of a large plaza. It was both breathtaking and confusing. Huge, it rose to a point along the front edifice in a style that looked flamboyant. I tried to count the spires that ran along the top, but stopped—there were far too many. Opening the guidebook, I saw I wasn't the first to call the cathedral "flamboyant." John Ruskin had made that observation as well. And there were over 135 spires.

The end result, though chaotic, was amazingly airy and delicate. As I stood there, reading about the history of the stone edifice, I heard bells begin to toll the hour. The sound didn't come from the cathedral—it came from nearby. It seemed to me that each full, deep tone, coming in measured increments, was summoning something malevolent into the plaza.

That sound instantly reignited my terror. I gasped, backed up, and fell into a fountain in the middle of the plaza. Pulling myself out and sitting on the edge of the fountain, ignoring the snickers of a young group of teenagers passing by, I wrung water from my clothes and rubbed at a small bruise forming on my leg.

Soft footfalls caught my attention. Looking up, I saw a tall, dark-haired man emerge from a nearby arcade. He was dressed in a tailored gray suit and expensive-looking leather shoes, and—despite the heat—carrying a black wool coat over one arm.

"Are you all right, Miss?" he inquired in a gentle, melodious voice.

I nodded, and then it struck me—not only had he had addressed me in English, but he looked as if he recognized me though I was sure I'd never seen him before.

Filled with dread, I slid off the rim of the fountain and joined a crowd of tourists. He walked a few steps closer then stopped and seemed content to stand and watch me walk away.

When the tour group stopped to listen to their guide, I turned and ran back across the square, ducking into crowds as best I could. It was the same feeling I'd gotten from the stranger in Chicago. I understood the fear the bookseller in Paris had shown, and Millicent as well, though she hadn't discussed it with me. There was something about these people, whoever they were, that were shadowing me—I felt dread when they approached.

I briefly wondered if they were even real or symptoms of paranoid delusion. If I could think that thought, I wasn't mentally ill. Correct?

I shook my head to clear it. I needed to get home and see a doctor. Why should these people be generating so much fear?

I caught a cab to the airport and stood in line at the ticket counter, trying to get on stand-by, so that I could leave immediately, but there were no flights to the U.S. out of Milan until the next morning.

Leaving the airport I fumed at myself and my nerves. The man had probably just guessed my nationality based on my appearance. Though I had bought some clothes in Italy, I was wearing a t-shirt and jeans, sneakers and a backpack, like the other teen-aged tourists I passed. I needed to get a grip.

I paced the city anxiously all evening, finally stopping at a cafe for supper, more to pass time than out of hunger. After glancing over the menu for a few minutes, I pointed at one of the listings, not caring what it was.

When the food came, I was relieved to find I'd ordered pasta with red sauce. I sat nervously at the wooden table on the street and barely picked at the plate of pasta. The waiter asked in broken English if my food was all right. He seemed so concerned about whether I liked his food that I burst into tears. It had been so long since I actually talked to someone—not since the book dealer in Paris.

The worried waiter went back into the café, reappearing a few minutes later with an older woman who sat with me for the rest of my meal. I suspected she was the owner though we couldn't really communicate. I ate a little more, which seemed to please her, and she looked at my postcard of the Last Supper. Together we watched people passing by in the growing dusk. At around 8:00 I paid the waiter, thanked them both as best I could, and left.

Tomorrow I would leave Europe and go back to Chicago, and I would go to school in the fall. I would be able to put these mysterious disappearances and spooky feelings behind me once I got home.

Back at my hotel, I realized I'd left my souvenir postcard of the Last Supper on the café table. I couldn't shake the feeling that I might have left my only chance of salvation behind with the kind waiter.

CHAPTER ELEVEN

The Flight Home

After yet another restless night I left for the airport. When I checked in for my flight, the stewardess said that my seat had been upgraded to First Class. I was surprised, but she added something about a large party and an overbooking. I wasn't convinced that I was getting the truth, but her English wasn't perfect, so I let it go. She raised an exquisitely groomed eyebrow at me when I said that I wasn't checking any luggage, but when I told her I had shipped the bags she nodded and gave me my boarding pass. On my way to the gate I bought another postcard of the Last Supper as well as several of the Milan Cathedral. I wrote notes to my family and a few friends. The storekeeper was willing to post them for a small fee, so I left them with him before going to my gate.

Waiting for my flight to be called, I felt like such a failure. How could I have turned the trip of a lifetime into a paranoid race across Europe? I tried not to dwell on my fear. As I glanced around, I saw a man outside the waiting area. He was dressed entirely in black and was leaning against the wall. He seemed to be staring at me though I couldn't see his eyes because of his black sunglasses. Dread threatened to suffocate me. I looked down at my lap and took a few deep breaths. When I glanced up, again, he was gone. *Right. Of course.*

I realized one reason the men I'd seen stood out from the crowd—in addition to being handsome—was because no one seemed to go near them. The man in Chicago, the man at the edge of the crowd in Paris...this most recent sighting.

Had they been there at all?

Maybe I was hallucinating. A trip to the doctor should help sort it all out. However terrifying the thought of madness, they had drugs for such things now. And those could end my fears. I opened my book, trying to shove those thoughts from my mind.

At last they called my flight.

Once I found my seat I settled in, luxuriating in the unaccustomed comfort of First Class. I was used to taking cheap flights. I carefully placed my book from the Parisian bookstore in the seat pocket in front of me, put in my ear buds, and waited for the flight to depart. Just as they were about to shut the door, a final passenger got on the plane.

As he made his way down the aisle, I recognized the tall, good-looking man as the solicitous stranger from the cathedral yesterday. Somehow this didn't surprise me. It had been a little too easy to leave Italy alone.

He took the seat next to me.

"Hello," he said, acting surprised to see me. "What a coincidence to meet you again. My name is Mr. Amalfi."

I was certain this wasn't a coincidence. But why would he have booked himself onto an international flight just to talk to me? I need to relax and get a grip. This was a long flight and I was stuck next to him.

Mr. Amalfi asked me about my trip and quickly got out of me that I was a student. Looking at my e-reader, he asked if I liked to read, and then he turned the conversation to bookstores. I sensed that he already knew about my trip to the bookstore in Paris.

I said I had visited bookstores looking for travel guides and had found one where the owner had shown me books on towns in the Italian countryside. He asked to see the text, so I pulled it out. He stroked the leather binding gently as he took it from me and held it in a proprietary manner. He opened it, and I noticed that it fell open to the same spot as when I read it in my hotel room. To the page on the Moltadano family.

"I am a collector of fine works," he said. "I would be very interested in purchasing this from you."

I told him that I had bought the book as a gift for a friend, and I wasn't willing to part with it. Mr. Amalfi wasn't buying my story.

I read a bit and pretended to go sleep in order to avoid talking to him. That worked until they brought dinner.

The stewardesses were very attentive to us throughout the flight. After all Mr. Amalfi was expensively dressed in addition to being incredibly handsome. He had an ethereal kind of beauty for a man. His skin was an unearthly pale, and his eyes were an odd, muddy brown with hints of red running through the irises. When they served dinner, he declined and said he had dined with friends before leaving Milan. He did accept a glass of wine, which he toyed with rather than drank, twirling the crystal expertly in his long, elegant fingers.

During our dinner conversation, I asked what brought him to Italy. He replied that he had been visiting friends in Milan.

I decided to try an aggressive tactic, to see if he really was antiquities dealer. I asked, "What made you want to be an art dealer?"

"I've always appreciated the beautiful and felt a need to conserve it. Some of the things I buy I restore and place in museums or public libraries where they become available again to the world," he said.

"Did you ever consider going into acting?" I said.

He looked startled and then shook his head, smiling. "People seem to think I am handsome but rarely phrase it that way. You are…different."

No, I am on to you.

CHAPTER TWELVE

Caught

The flight passed, and soon I saw land on the horizon of the blue Atlantic. I asked Mr. Amalfi more questions as I hoped to find clues to support my suspicions that he knew about Millicent. So I asked him about his business, what college he had attended, even questions about his family.

But I didn't get past his smooth exterior. He was a good listener and an expert at turning the conversation back to me. I answered the usual questions, which focused on stories about growing up in the suburbs of Chicago and spending summers with my grandparents in Michigan. He laughed at my stories about my younger siblings and the scrapes they could get into at the dunes and while blueberry picking. I was finding it hard to dislike such a flattering and attentive listener, but I kept focused on the missing Millicent.

I noticed he kept his eye on my purloined book. I opened it again, hoping to get a response from him. The only response was that he quit looking at it.

We arrived in New York, and Mr. Amalfi and I got off the plane together and headed for luggage and customs.

Now that I was back in the United States, I decided to be bold. Though I had only my suspicions to go on, I was certain this man knew something. I decided to take his picture and send it to one of the investigators in the Alderwoman's office where my mother worked. Back home, I would ask them to check him out for me. Was he really a licensed antiquities dealer? Did he have a case with Millicent's law firm?

I bent to mess with my shoelaces and tried to take Mr. Amalfi's picture with my iPhone when I thought he wasn't looking. He turned his head at the last second though, and something dangerous flashed behind his eyes. I backed away from him instinctively, and the look was gone.

He put a smile back onto his face and gallantly offered to carry my bags for me. I didn't have any, which he clearly thought was odd. I didn't care. I finally felt I had something that might be a clue to Millicent's disappearance, but I didn't know what to do. Should I call Millicent's partner, Mr. Gupta? Call that investigator, Mike?

After we cleared customs, we walked to the arrivals gate. A man in a chauffeur's cap was waiting for him with his luggage.

"Welcome back. Did you have a nice trip, sir?" he asked.

"Thank you, Duane," Mr. Amalfi said. Turning to me he asked, "Can I give you a lift somewhere?"

He had a driver. Of course. "No, I'll just take the train," I replied. I didn't want him to know I was catching a connecting flight. "I'll be fine."

"As you wish," he said with a touch of regret and walked out the sliding glass doors.

I ducked into the restroom, wanting to make sure he was gone. I spent a few minutes brushing my hair and washing my face. Finally I headed back outside.

As I exited, I looked right and left down the long corridor and felt relieved when I didn't see the handsome man waiting for me.

As I stepped back into the terminal, I was pulled against someone's chest, and a chilly hand covered my mouth. I tried to fight, seeking to reach his eyes with my thumbs, but my nostrils were pinched shut and my mouth held closed.

Soon all was black, and I saw nothing.

Captive

I woke up on the floor of an unfamiliar but ordinary-looking room. There was a bed with a gold and black patterned bedspread, a stained yellow carpet on the floor, and an inexpensive wooden dresser with a large television on top. It was like a room in a cheap hotel except that there were no windows.

I tried the door. It was locked, of course. I attempted to summon help, first calling "Hello" and then yelling "Help!" but there was no answer. I kicked and banged on the door but still no response. Only silence. Finally I lay down on the bed, pulling my legs to my chest, wondering how I'd come to this. I was just a college student who had been traveling in Europe. What had happened?

After a few hours Mr. Amalfi's driver, Duane, came to the door. I opened my mouth to scream, but he flashed to my side at inhuman speed. He covered my mouth with one hand and whispered, "Shall I suffocate you again, or will you be silent?"

Terrified, I nodded. He took his hand from my mouth and pulled me to my feet. As before, I noticed that his hand was cold, and he was very strong. He walked me out of the room into the hallway then opened the fire exit stairwell door. We went down two flights of metal stairs. At the bottom he opened a metal door and looked outside while holding me behind him in a painful grip. Once he seemed satisfied, he led me into an alleyway where an expensive-looking black car with tinted windows was waiting. As we stepped outside, someone turned the motor on.

He opened the car door, put his hand on top of my head, pushed it down, and shoved me into the backseat.

Once inside I fumbled for a seat belt, and the man in the driver's seat laughed. I said nothing and automatically buckled the belt. I was terrified, sure that they were taking me some place to kill me. I kept my head down but tried to slyly peek out the window so I could figure out where we were headed. No luck, as the windows were tinted so darkly that I couldn't make out any details.

To my surprise we drove to an airport and boarded a small private plane.

Once on the plane, Duane gestured me toward a seat. I sat and once again buckled myself in. It looked well-maintained as the seats and the floor were clean. The shades were pulled over all the windows. I was tempted to lift mine up, but I kept still.

We were the only passengers, and after a few minutes we took off. As we taxied down the runway, Duane looked out his window, so I took the opportunity to examine him. He was in his early twenties, tall and good-looking. He wasn't overly muscular but quite trim and fit. He hadn't taken off the sunglasses he had been wearing since he met Mr. Amalfi in the airport. Once the plane was off the ground, he glanced over at me, and I looked back down at my lap.

I hadn't eaten since that meal on the flight from Italy, so about thirty minutes into the flight, I told him, "I'm thirsty."

"So am I," he answered with a smirk.

Chills went up my spine, and I shivered and slid lower in my seat.

His smirk changed to a grin, but he got up and went to the galley at the front of the plane. I heard him rustling around, and he returned shortly with several small bottles of water and packages of peanuts.

I took them gratefully. "Thanks."

He nodded his head, pulled out a laptop, and typed on it.

I ate the nuts quietly. Since he was focused on his computer, I spent a few more minutes studying him. I could see muscles under his tailored, blue button-down shirt. His slacks looked like they were part of a suit, and I noticed a suit jacket folded over the back of one of the seats. Had he been carrying that when we got on? I shuddered, realizing I couldn't remembered any details of being moved from the car to the plane.

"Where are we going?" I finally asked.

He looked over at me but didn't answer.

"What do you want with me?" I pressed.

This time he shut the computer and stared at me for a few seconds. Finally his lips twitched upward, and he said, "You'll find out soon enough."

My skin crawled at this response, and I shrank back in my seat. I didn't ask anything else.

Time ceased to have any meaning for me. I curled up in my seat, closing my eyes to try to sleep. After what seemed like a day, but was probably only a few hours, the plane circled for a landing. I cautiously lifted the window shade and peeked out the window in an attempt to figure out where we were.

I didn't recognize this landscape. The ground below looked flat and desolate though I saw a few sprawling, wooden buildings. Ranches maybe? I couldn't tell.

After landing, Duane opened the door and jumped down from the plane. I saw him wheeling a metal stair-case to the plane. As I stood in the open doorway, I saw we were on the far edge of a small airport, nowhere near the control tower or hangars. As I walked down the metal stairs to the deserted airstrip, no attempt was made to keep me quiet. No one would hear me scream.

At the foot of the stairs Duane grabbed me by the wrist and led me to a black car that was waiting on the tarmac. When he opened the door, I quickly got inside. I didn't want to be pushed again. Looking behind me I saw a pilot leave our plane and push the metal staircase to a container at the side of the landing strip. I shuddered to think they must do this a lot.

I buckled my seat belt and leaned back in the seat. Who were these men? They moved with incredible speed and strength. What secret were they protecting? My conversation with Amalfi on the plane seemed innocent enough. I hadn't learned anything about him, and I thought my questions were more those of a nosy fellow-passenger despite my intentions. But I had obviously alarmed him. My only thought was that Millicent had found out something that someone didn't want her to know. After taking her they'd become interested in me for the same reason.

As the driver pulled onto the main road, I studied the scenery on either side of the road, looking for landmarks, but saw only the barren landscape.

CHAPTER FOURTEEN

The Big House

We turned off the main highway and pulled onto an unpaved dirt road that was nearly imperceptible from the highway. Once we passed a slight hill, the road became paved again, and a block of gray cinderblock buildings came into view. They were long and low, like warehouses, but for some reason, I thought of holding cells. I noticed with a shudder that the windows were barred. Was this where I was headed?

Passing these, we turned into a landscaped area. Tall, graceful trees and rows of shrubs, all carefully trimmed and tended, lined the road. I noticed they blocked the view of the cinderblock buildings. Then we were pulling onto an elegant circular driveway in front of a colonial style, three-story mansion built of red brick.

We stopped in front of the portico where four columns supported a gable. Duane got out and reappeared at my door. I never saw him move. He hauled me out of the car roughly by the wrist, and I yelped. He loosened his grip but pushed me ahead of him up the porch steps and in the front door.

We entered a dimly lit hallway. A woman wearing a blue maid's uniform was on her hands and knees scrubbing the marble floor with a brush. She didn't make eye contact.

Duane held my shoulder with an iron grasp which almost crushed my shoulder blade. I gasped in pain. He eased his grip and walked next to me, directing me up a sweeping stairway which split at a middle landing. There, stairs branched right and left under a stained glass, gabled window. He turned us to the left, and we walked down a hallway past several doorways.

He knocked on a closed door then waited a few seconds before opening it and shoving me inside a room. It was deathly quiet inside, and it took a few seconds for my eyes to adjust to the dim light. I nervously scanned the room. Even in the gloom, I could tell we were in an elegant office. Opposite the door there was a fireplace and a small leather sofa with a few chairs arranged next to it. A man was sitting behind the large antique desk that dominated the room. Pushing me into one of the chairs next to the fireplace, Duane went to the man sitting behind the desk.

They had a quiet exchange of words, and while they were talking, the door opened and a man wearing a white coat and carrying a black medical bag entered the room. I felt relieved. If this were a doctor maybe he would help me.

My relief was short-lived. The newcomer looked first at me and then at the man sitting at the desk.

"Just the usual, then quarantine before we send her to the barracks. She's new," was all the seated man said.

The doctor nodded and pulled up one of the leather chairs next to mine then sat down beside me, turning on a light on the end table next to my chair. It was very bright, but the lampshade kept it from shining in my eyes.

Pulling my arm onto the table, he inspected it, tapping until he found a vein. As he leaned closer, I was hit with the stale smell of alcohol on his breath. My heart sank.

Seeming satisfied, he leaned back, rummaged in his bag, and pulled out a small rubber tube. He took my arm to tie a tourniquet, but I yanked it back.

"What are you doing?" I demanded.

Instantly Duane was in front of us. He grabbed my arm, pushed it back on the table, and held it in a bruising grip.

I winced in pain, and the doctor looked at him. "You can let go. She won't move again, right?" the doctor said as he looked at me. His speech was slurred.

I nodded, too frightened to speak, and my arm was released.

"I'm going to draw some blood prior to quarantine," he told me. "Standard procedure here. Nothing to worry about."

I knew I had a lot to worry about.

CHAPTER FIFTEEN

Quarantine

The doctor drew two large tubes of blood and then released the tourniquet. He scrubbed the blood off my arm thoroughly with an alcohol wipe before covering the wound with a Band-Aid. "Press that tightly," he advised me, "and flush the Band-Aid down the toilet after thirty minutes."

I nodded, and then he packed his bag. To my surprise, he placed one tube on the desk before putting the other in his black bag.

After he left, Duane pulled me out of the chair. As he ushered me from the room, I saw the other man pick up the tube from the desk and pull out the cork stopper. The heavy door closed firmly behind us.

Leading me back down the stairs, Duane turned down a hallway at the foot of the staircase. Unlike the grand entryway and central staircase, this hallway looked more like a utility corridor, a concrete tunnel without any attempt at decoration, painted a cool, industrial green. A short distance down this hall, he opened a door and shoved me into a room.

"See you in a few days," he said with a malicious smirk as he closed the door.

I wasn't surprised to hear the sound of a key being turned in the lock.

Relieved to be away from him, I leaned against the door and looked around. The room was sterile, like a hospital room. There were no curtains on the windows, which were made of a frosted glass that allowed some light in without allowing a view of the outside.

Nearby was a rickety plastic chair. I finished my exam of the room and sat down. I felt shaky, whether from fear or blood loss, I wasn't sure.

There was a metal bed against one wall under one of the frosted window. I was horrified to see the bedrails had wrist restraints permanently attached. After a few minutes, I got up to inspect it more closely. The bed had a blue, waffle-weave blanket that looked as if it had been washed and bleached many times, stretched over scratchy white sheets. A thin pillow in a worn, but clean pillow case lay at the top.

The attached bathroom had no door. I flushed the Band-Aid as the doctor had instructed. The room contained a white sink with exposed metal pipes underneath, a small mirror, toilet, and shower stall. There was no shower curtain, and the shower rod had been re-moved.

At least I was alone.

A few hours later the door was unlocked, and a middle-aged woman in a maid uniform entered with a tray of food. She set it at the foot of the bed without raising her eyes.

I saw a name embroidered on her uniform.

"Thank you, Betty," I said softly.

She nodded and left, still without having met my eyes.

CHAPTER SIXTEEN

End of Quarantine

From the number of meals, I guessed three days had passed. I tried to sleep, but my sleep was disrupted with nightmares about all that had happened since that day in June in Chicago. My waking thoughts were the same relentless parade—the mysterious stranger, the Parisian bookseller, the art dealer from the plane—all leading up to my kidnapping.

I got used to Betty's silent presence. She never spoke. She brought in a new tray and left with the old one, never meeting my eyes. Still, her daily appearances reassured me. The food consisted of sandwiches, baby carrots, and some kind of wrapped dessert for lunch and dinner, and cold cereal with milk and fruit in the morning. Though the food wasn't appetizing, I ate it. I needed the strength.

Finally, the moment I dreaded arrived. Duane opened the door. When I saw him, I unconsciously

shifted away from him; he smiled as if enjoying my reaction.

"Time to go," he said.

I got up quickly, not wanting to give him the opportunity to further damage my bruised wrist. Glancing
around, I realized I was reluctant to leave the room. It
had been a prison, but I didn't know what lay ahead.

He stepped outside the door and gestured impatient-
ly, so I moved to his side. As we walked down the green
concrete hallway, I saw a familiar figure. A tall man with
brown hair to his shoulders leaned against the wall. He
wasn't wearing a coat or hat, but I was sure it was the
man from Chicago. He had the same confident stance—
back against the wall, one knee up, arms folded across
his chest.

The stranger must have said something too low for
me to hear because Duane hissed and shoved me behind
his back, crouching low in front of me, arms stretched
out on either side.

"Duane," the man from Chicago said in a warning
tone.

The stranger quickly moved his own body to imitate
Duane's position, and they circled one another until, in
an action too fast for my eyes, Duane was left lying on
his back on the floor, howling with an inhuman sound,
staring at what remained of his left arm.

His forearm, hand still attached, lay on the floor in front of him.

I was stunned to see that no blood came from his arm, only a white substance that frothed a little as it dripped off the end of his stump.

No blood? Where was the blood?

I staggered back, feeling for the wall behind me. My legs were unable to support my weight. I slid down, gasping for breath, overcome with terror.

Instantly, the stranger was standing over me, looking down with a stony expression. As I looked up, I saw that his eyes were bright red.

There's the blood, I thought before everything went black.

CHAPTER SEVENTEEN

The Stranger

I don't know how long I was out, but I still felt shaky when I woke. Patting my hands experimentally around me while my eyes were still closed, I realized I was lying on a sofa. I smelled the tell-tale scent of stale alcohol, so I wasn't surprised when I opened my eyes and saw the doctor leaning over me.

He stood upright as I turned toward him. Putting away his stethoscope, he said to someone I couldn't see, "She's all right. Just shock."

Glancing around, I recognized the office I'd been brought to the first day. The same man sat behind the desk. As I sat up, I felt a strong, cold hand on my shoulder. "Wait a moment," a voice said. It was cool yet authoritative like the art dealer Mr. Amalfi.

Looking up, I saw the stranger from Chicago. It was definitely him. I recognized his strong, handsome features and the brown hair that came to his shoulders. He held my eyes steadily with his own. My gaze locked on his red irises. Were red eyes like his hidden by the sunglasses I had seen on the other strangers? He looked over at the doctor, who just nodded.

"Will she be okay to travel?" asked the stranger.

"Yes, Mr. Samuels," replied the doctor. "She'll be fine. Just make sure she gets plenty of fluids though."

Mr. Samuels helped me to my feet and noticed when I winced as I extended my arm. He pulled back my sleeve and began to inspect one the bruises Duane had left on my arm. His eyes shot over to the doctor.

"I didn't do that," the doctor said, appearing to choose his words carefully.

"Duane," Mr. Samuels hissed.

"It's possible. You must watch your strength around these girls," the doctor replied.

Mr. Samuels nodded and put his arm around my back, appearing to be assessing whether I could stand on my own.

"Can you walk or do I need to carry you?" he asked me.

I didn't want him to touch me, so I struggled to stay on my feet, holding on to the sofa for support.

After watching me for a moment, he said, "All right then, let's go," as he waved me toward the door.

Considering what I had just seen him do to Duane a few minutes earlier, I obeyed. I walked to the door, and he followed, touching my shoulder lightly to guide me.

As we left the office, I saw the man behind the desk watching me thoughtfully, stroking his chin with his hand. He looked disappointed. As the door closed, I saw him filing some papers into a desk drawer. Glancing up, he caught my eye. A frown flashed across his face, and his mouth twisted into a snarl.

In that instant, he didn't look completely human.

Walking the familiar hallway with Mr. Samuels, I didn't see any signs of Duane. There was a puddle of white that appeared to have stained and partially burnt the floor at the spot where the two had fought. I skirted the stain carefully which amused my escort, and he flashed a tight smile which quickly vanished.

We made our way down the stairs in silence.

At the foot of the stairs, I saw a familiar figure standing by the front door, her head bowed. On the floor next to her was a bucket and mop. I remembered that someone had been cleaning the floor the day I first entered the house with Duane. It must have been she.

"Good-bye, Betty, and thank you," I said softly.

CHAPTER EIGHTEEN

The Mystery Man

I heard a low growl from Mr. Samuels after I spoke to Betty. Startled, I kept my head down and waited to be told what to do next.

He led me out into the bright sunlight. I paused on the porch, blinking and waiting for my eyes to adjust after spending three days indoors. A black Audi with tinted windows waited in the driveway.

Opening the back door, Mr. Samuels guided me in. A tall man with black hair sitting in the driver's seat looked at me in the rearview mirror. His eyes were bright red, too. They narrowed when he caught me looking at him, and I focused on fastening the seatbelt and didn't look again. Mr. Samuels got in front on the passenger side.

The car began moving as soon as he closed his door. We were on the same road I had traveled a few days before. I looked out the window as we moved down the landscaped driveway and past the gray cinderblock buildings, and I wondered once again what was kept in the bunkers. On the highway the two men in the front seat spoke in voices too low for me understand. We made the drive back to the airport quickly.

The driver pulled directly onto the runway under the wing of a private plane. Mr. Samuels didn't bother moving a metal staircase—he simply picked me up with one arm and leapt to the open door of the plane. I gasped in surprise at the sudden movement as the plane door was at least fifteen feet from the ground. Looking around, I realized that his jump had been shielded from the sight of the tower and hangars by the body of the plane. They probably only used the staircase when they thought someone might be watching.

The interior of the plane was posh. There were cream-colored leather chairs arranged in a conversational floor plan instead of the usual rows. He carried me to a seat and set me down. To my surprise I was still clinging to his shirt after the terrifying leap. I let go, horrified to realize that I was holding onto him, and he smirked.

What was he? Either I was completely nuts or he was some kind of a non-human being. Both possibilities were terrifying. Was I caught inside a world of paranoid hallucinations? This man had ripped off Duane's arm, after moving faster than my eye could follow, and just now leapt effortlessly from the tarmac into a plane while carrying me. Plus he had those freaky red eyes.

I thought about the blood drawn by the doctor, and my mind went back to the bookseller trying to hide the book about vampires in Paris. If they were vampires, what was going to happen to me?

Insanity seemed a better alternative. Maybe there were drugs for my condition.

I was forced back to this reality, however surreal, when I saw the second man had jumped onto the plane and was closing the door. After sealing the door, he entered the cockpit. Mr. Samuels went up to the cockpit door, and they exchanged a few words; then he shut the door and came back to sit opposite me.

Mr. Samuels stared at me for a moment then stood up and took a briefcase out of an overhead bin. Pulling up a tray table from beside the seat, he opened and then tapped away on a laptop and did not pay any more attention to me for the rest of the short flight.

As we began to descend, I looked out the window to get a sense of where we were. We flew over several small cities; between the cities there was open land broken up by rock outcroppings alongside a river.

We soon landed on the short runway of a rural airport. Gray hangars with numbers on the top lined one end of the runway, and a forest surrounded the other three sides. Once on the ground, we were met by a slender brunette waiting beside a black SUV.

No one had spoken to me since we left the mansion in the middle of nowhere.

After getting in the car, I fell asleep despite my fear, lulled by the gentle motion of the vehicle.

I woke up to find Mr. Samuels carrying me, my legs draped over his hard arms. I started and began to struggle.

Red eyes looked down at me, and I froze. He smiled at my reaction and set me down on the bed in a large bedroom. I pulled away from him, and he watched me, amused.

"The bathroom is over there," he said, pointing to the left. "Get some sleep."

He paused in the open doorway, his lean figure outlined in the hallway light.

"Where are we?" I asked in a voice that I'd hoped would be stronger.

"Home," he said simply, then shut the door.

I was surprised not to hear a key turn in the lock.

Once my eyes adjusted to the dim light, I examined the room beginning with the windows next to the bed. They weren't locked though they had heavy screens. Looking outside, I saw I was on the second story of a large house. A wide back yard extended around the back of the house in a sweeping circle, bordered by a forest. I couldn't see any other houses, but they might have been blocked by the trees. The door opened behind me, and I turned to see Mr. Samuels in the doorway.

"Do I need to nail those shut?" he asked.

"Just getting some air, that's all," I replied as I pulled back from the window.

My answer seemed to satisfy him, as he closed the door.

CHAPTER NINETEEN

First Morning

When the door closed, I went to bed, only taking off my shoes before crawling under the covers. The room around the bed was full of dark shapes with darker shadows behind them. I knew it was furniture, but the effect was spooky.

I'd scarcely closed my eyes when I woke up to bright sunlight coming in the window.

My mouth felt dry and nasty. A bottle of water was on the bedside table. It hadn't been there the night before. I drank it in bed.

In the morning light, the room looked quite normal. The bed was a heavy walnut four-poster, covered by a thick, white bedspread with a traditional patterned texture with several quilts between the spread and the white cotton sheets. A matching dresser and wardrobe rounded out the set. The pieces looked antique. There was a small marble-top washstand with a large pitcher and bowl on it, and a metal bar holding a towel on the lower right side. I had seen these sort of furnishings in older homes of my elderly relatives in Michigan. Braided oval rugs lay in front of each piece of furniture, just like in my great-grandmother's house.

I got up and went into to the bathroom. A white terrycloth robe hung from a wooden hook behind the door, so I took off my clothes and slipped it on. Feeling vulnerable, I waited for a moment, but no one came in, and I felt bolder. I started the shower water and paused again, listening, then stepped into the shower.

As I stood under the spout, I listened carefully for any sounds of the door being opened, but at last relaxed and let the jets of hot water work on the tense muscles of my back. I scrubbed myself thoroughly using the bar of white soap that was in the holder and finally turned off the water.

I wrapped myself in a towel as I stepped out and was surprised at how these simple everyday acts made me feel stronger. I was pulling the bathroom drawers open, looking for a hairbrush, when I heard the door open behind me.

I saw Mr. Samuels's reflection in the mirror and froze. If he were really a vampire, why could I see him in the mirror? There was obviously much I didn't know about this strange world I was trapped in.

He walked in, looking over my shoulder at my reflection appraisingly as I pulled the towel tighter and reached for the bathrobe. His eyes stopped on the bruise on my shoulder from where Duane had grabbed me, and he put out his hand to prevent me picking up the robe.

He was much taller than I. I stood still as he came to stand directly behind me. He seemed to be doing an assessment of the bruises on my body, from my shoulder to the faint one on my leg from when I'd fallen into the fountain in Milan.

I heard a soft noise to my left and noticed the woman from the night before had slipped in beside him as well. This morning her hair was in a simple braid, and she wore a blue print dress belted at the waist.

"Any bruises under that towel that I can't see?" he asked after a tense moment.

I pulled the towel tighter and shook my head.

He took my bruised wrist in one hand and carefully turned it. His hands, though cold, were gentle.

"Will you get her some ice for this?" he said to the woman.

She said yes and disappeared.

Finished with his inspection of me, Mr. Samuels reached to touch my wet hair. I pulled away from his hand and looked down at the sink, grabbing it tightly.

Silence filled the room. I felt my heart would burst from fear. What was he going to do that he wanted that woman out of the room?

He finally said, "Lillian left some clothes on the bed. Come downstairs and eat when you're dressed."

He left the bathroom, closing the door behind him. When he was gone, I tried to catch my breath and realized I was shaking. After a moment, when my hands were steadier, I looked for a hair dryer. I didn't see one, so I just combed my hair out after toweling it dry.

Back in the bedroom, I found khaki shorts and a white short-sleeved top on the bed. I dressed, took a deep breath, went to the door and stepped into the hall. I was standing on the second floor of a large house, nicely furnished with exposed wood floors and framed photographs of wildlife scenes on the walls. It looked quite normal, like an expensive hunting lodge, not a place where people were kept prisoner.

I stood still and listened for any sounds.

The house was silent as a tomb.

CHAPTER TWENTY

My Food

I ventured downstairs, and before I reached the first floor, Lillian appeared at the foot of the stairs. She didn't say anything, just waited for me and then guided me toward the back of the house.

Along the way we passed several closed doors and a wide doorway that led into the living room. The room had traditional leather furniture in masculine tones along with wood-paneled walls and bare wood floors. A large fireplace with a framed deer head over the mantle dominated the room, and somewhere a clock was ticking, the only noise I heard besides my own footsteps. Passing the living room, I heard the sound of gears moving, and the clock chimed.

By the time it reached its fifth chime, we'd entered the kitchen. Glancing around, I took in the tiled floors, a pegboard on one wall that held pots and pans, and wooden counters under the cabinets. It was traditionally laid out, built before kitchen islands were common.

Lillian seemed to relax in this room.

"What would you like for breakfast?" she asked in a low, melodious voice. She spoke with a slight accent, one I couldn't quite place. It sounded rural American. Though I hadn't traveled much, I had cousins from Virginia and Mississippi. The soft cadence of her voice sounded similar.

"I can fix myself something. I don't want to put you to any trouble," I replied.

She gestured to the stainless steel refrigerator, and I opened it.

"Stocked with about everything I can remember your people eat," she said from behind me.

I froze at the "your people," but quickly recovered enough to rummage inside.

The refrigerator was spotless, as if it had never been used. The French doors held a variety of unopened bottles. The crisper held bags of vegetables and fruit, and there were packages of meat and cheeses as well. I found juice, eggs, and bread, and I pulled those out. Lillian didn't say anything, so I took a pan from the pegboard and filled it with water to boil the eggs.

She seemed content to just watch, leaning against the counter.

"Your people?" I finally asked.

"Human," she stated simply.

If I had been holding anything, I would have dropped it. It's one thing to think something, another to have it confirmed by someone. I took a second to recover, and then reminded myself that I needed to eat in order to think clearly. After that I could figure out where I was and how to escape.

I opened drawers, looking for a butter knife, and felt Lillian's hand on the back of mine. It was cold, just like Duane and Mr. Samuels's. I glanced at her, startled.

"What are you looking for?" she asked in a slow drawl, not quite Southern, but close.

"A knife to butter my toast with," I replied.

"I'll handle those," she said, pulling out a knife which she laid on the counter.

I just nodded and stood by the sink while I waited for the water to boil. She went to the window, lifting the curtain, and while she was gazing into the backyard, I took the opportunity to look around the room carefully. Kitchens did have weapons or things that could be used as weapons. I made a mental list of the possibilities— knives, boiling water, even heavy objects. Like the rest of the house, the kitchen had a rustic feel despite having new appliances including an expensive stove and refrigerator. The cupboards were wood with glass doors displaying their contents. The large pegboard held a variety of pans. Unlike the rest of the kitchen, these pans didn't look new. They were cast iron, remnants of another era.

Lillian dropped the curtain and leaned against the wall in silence, looking at her fingernails. Once the food was ready, I found a plate and sat down to eat.

A shadow fell across the table, and Mr. Samuels stood in the kitchen. I hadn't heard him enter.

"Would you like something to eat?" I asked though neither he nor Lillian were showing any interest in the food I had just prepared.

He looked at me and replied, "I don't think you and I will be dining together."

CHAPTER TWENTY-ONE

Red Meat

I needed to eat—I had to stay sharp to try to escape or find a way to call for help. As I ate, the room was so quiet that I thought the sound I made crunching my toast would rattle the pots on the pegboard. When I finished, I pushed back my chair without looking at my silent companions.

I washed my dishes and hung the towel on the rack. Mr. Samuels and Lillian had been sitting at the table while I ate, but when I turned around after washing the dishes, I saw that Mr. Samuels had left the room as silently as he'd entered.

Lillian turned to me and said, "There's some books in the library. Maybe you can find something to read."

"Thank you," I replied. Maybe I could find an ally in Lillian.

The library was the second room from the kitchen behind one of the closed doors. The room was lined to the ceiling with built-in bookshelves. The spines ranged from paperbacks to older, leather-bound works.

A sofa and chairs were arranged in front of a large fireplace with a mantle made of stones set in white mortar. In addition to floor lamps with beaded lampshades, sconces with tan shades lined the walls. The exposed pine floor was covered with old-fashioned braided rugs, just as in the bedroom upstairs. The rugs looked handmade and reminded me of rugs I had seen in an Amish market. Rag rugs, I remembered.

As I searched the bookcase, Lillian sat down on the sofa and pulled clothing from a basket on the floor. She worked in silence, mending shirts and darning socks while I searched the bookcases. I found a few books that looked interesting and nodded to her when I was done. She put her mending basket into a trunk beside the sofa, and we went back up to my room.

Once I was inside, she turned around and made her silent way back down the stairs. I sat down in the chair to read. But I found that the one activity I always used to escape from real life wasn't enough to distract me from the quiet terror of my situation. I got up and went to the window. I noted again that we were in a rural area with a forest bordering the property. I struggled to find any clue that could give me a hint to where this house was. The trees were deciduous, but I had never been good with tree identification. I tried to remember the difference between maples, oaks, and elms, but all I could remember was that they were all tall trees that shed their leaves in the winter. Maybe I would find a book on trees in that library downstairs.

The backyard was well-maintained. It covered a broad area and wasn't fenced. I could see there was a screened porch to the left below my window, and I guessed my room was over the kitchen. I didn't see any roads or any other houses—only tree-covered bluffs in the distance.

The morning quickly turned to noon. Lillian came back and knocked on the door at lunch time, taking me back downstairs.

Lunch was a quiet meal, and I was glad Mr. Samuels didn't join us this time.

I was cleaning up after the grilled cheese sandwich I had made when Lillian asked about dinner. I told her I usually made an omelet or frittata for supper.

"I've got some nice roast beef for sandwiches or some turkey," she commented. "Are you sure you wouldn't like a hot roast beef sandwich?"

Though I appreciated that she was being solicitous, I answered, "I'm a vegetarian. I don't eat meat."

She gave me an odd look but nodded and escorted me back to my room.

That evening, Lillian pulled a steak out of the fridge and took it to the stove. As she turned on the broiler, I decided to remind her about my diet.

"That looks wonderful, but I'm vegetarian," I told her as I went to the fridge to get something else.

I turned to see Mr. Samuels had entered the room behind me.

"You're going to eat red meat," he said calmly.

"Thank you, but no, it's against my principles as a vegetarian," I replied, scared but deciding to hold my ground.

"Those 'principles' you refer to are not a luxury I am going to allow. You need the iron, so you will eat it."

Lillian put the steak in the broiler as he and I spoke. As I looked at him, I felt my resistance begin to falter. Finally I sat down at the table. He never allowed me to break eye contact. I was trapped under his gaze. I couldn't look away.

"Dinner's ready," Lillian said as she took the steak off the heat and put it on a plate in front of me.

When her arm briefly moved in front of me, I was able to break free of his piercing gaze. I looked down at my plate and pushed it away.

"You're hungry, aren't you?" Mr. Samuels said brusquely. Against my will, I looked up at him, and he caught my eye. Unable to break away, I stared into his red eyes. I felt hungry. Very hungry and ready to eat anything.

He cut up the meat with a steak knife and pushed it across the plate.

"Eat it," he commanded. A piece at a time, I slowly put it in my mouth, chewed, and swallowed. He had hypnotized me, and I couldn't break his grip.

Finally, the steak was done. He released me from his gaze, and I stared down at my lap for a few seconds before looking up. "What just happened?" I asked.

"You were feeling my hunger," he answered succinctly.

I sat still for a moment and tried to make sense of what just happened. How had he done that?

"If you're hungry, why don't you have something?" I asked, attempting to establish some kind of relationship.

"I fully intend to feed, and soon. The level of hunger you just experienced is a daily occurrence for us. It isn't strong enough for me to be ready to feed," he replied, staring across the table at me.

When he left the room, I broke down sobbing. Lillian washed the dishes behind me without saying a word.

I knew I hadn't yet experienced the worst this house had in store for me.

CHAPTER TWENTY-TWO

His Food

I rarely left my room. I could feel tension growing by the day.

I went to the kitchen at meal times without waiting for Lillian. It allowed me a few seconds alone in the hallway to look for a phone and get a better feel for the house. On one of those trips I decided to try the front door. I knew Mr. Samuels was fast, but I had been getting to the kitchen without meeting Lillian, so I figured I might have a few seconds before he would come into the hall. So one morning I turned toward the front door instead of the kitchen when I reached the foot of the stairs.

Instantly, Mr. Samuels was in front of me, leaning against the door. His arms were folded in front of his chest, and his head was turned to one side as he regarded me steadily with an impassive look.

I froze.

"Lock the door to your room or shackle you to the bed?" he asked. "Which one were you looking for?"

"Just going to check that squeaky board on the front porch. I can hear when someone's outside," I snapped back

Silence stretched between us for a few seconds while I waited for his reaction. The only sound was my breath dragging through my mouth and into and out of my lungs. I had surprised both of us with my bravado.

His lips turned upwards into a slight smile, but it disappeared, and his face went stony again.

I turned toward the kitchen but stumbled as the sudden wave of bravery that had allowed me to stand up to him vanished. Lillian was at my side instantly and helped me to the kitchen.

The next morning when I came downstairs, Mr. Samuels stunned me by suddenly appearing and shoving me up against the wall, tilting my head back as he sniffed my neck.

I gasped in surprise and terror and tried to push him away using all my strength. He ignored my efforts. It was like shoving a marble statue. He sank his teeth into the left side of my throat. I screamed from both the sharp pain and shock.

Is this it? Is this my death?

Fear surged through me. I felt him growl and begin to suck at the wound. He lifted me in his arms so he wouldn't have to stoop and held me in place by pinning me to the wall with his body. As he leaned against me, the weight of his body was so great that I felt my ribcage being crushed. I couldn't breathe and heard a crack from inside as if a rib had broken.

As he guzzled, I began to feel light-headed. I closed my eyes and continued to push at him, fighting this death any way I could, though I realized I was helpless to stop him.

But it seemed he wasn't ready to kill me yet. He released me after a minute.

"The smell of your fear makes you taste even better," he whispered as he pulled back, licking my blood off his lips.

When he let go, I slipped down the wall and winced in pain as I desperately tried to suck air into my bruised rib cage. He caught me before I hit the floor and held my shoulder so that I slid into a sitting position against the wall as he held me upright with his knee. Eventually I stopped sliding and stayed in one place with my knees clutched to my chest as I tried to catch my breath. Once I was still, he left and went into his office.

I closed my eyes, petrified from fright. I was still alive. But for how much longer? After a few minutes I tried to get up but felt too woozy. Lillian appeared and knelt next to me; her cool hands pulling me to my feet with surprising gentleness.

"I heard that rib crack from the other room," she muttered. "Can you breathe?"

I nodded, doubling over as the pain asserted itself.

She carried me upstairs, lifting me easily despite her size, and helped me into bed before disappearing. Desperately afraid of being alone, I reached out instinctively toward the one person in the house who had helped me, but I pulled my hand back. She was, I reminded myself, my jailer. She reappeared moments later with orange juice and crackers. I downed the juice and crackers quickly, then turned away from her and sobbed as I clutched my sore side.

They really were vampires.

The stories in the book I found in Paris were true. Those men that I had been getting that warning sense from while traveling, they must have all been vampires. Were there really so many of them? They had been everywhere, in France and Italy as well as in Chicago. How could they keep their status as mere myths and legends? Then it occurred to me that anybody who took them seriously, like Millicent—and now me—simply disappeared.

As I struggled with these realizations, Lillian gently pulled one of the quilts over me and left, turning out the light before she quietly closed the door.

I dozed off but soon woke again because I was having trouble breathing. Lillian returned and helped me sit up. "Let me see your side," she said.

I moved the bedding out of the way for her exam. After she lifted up my t-shirt gently and touched my side, she called out, "Mack." Mr. Samuels instantly appeared by my bed.

I shrank away from him, but he pulled me back, holding my eyes with his own. He probed my side, and I winced. He noticed and gentled his touch. After running his fingers along my side and back he stood up.

"It's just bruised. You'll be fine," he said. "I'll be more careful next time."

I had never heard more terrible words.

CHAPTER TWENTY-THREE

His Family

He'd said the scent of my fear was intoxicating, so I decided to discourage him. I might not be able to stop the rush of fear when he grabbed me, but I could hold my head up and walk the gauntlet with dignity.

He caught on to what I was doing, and the second time I made it to the stairs without looking to the right or left, I heard a low growl from his office.

Good. I just deprived him of a little treat. No taste of fear from me on that trip. It was a small victory, but I took what I could get. For now, until I could get my hands on a weapon.

As the weeks went by, Mack would stalk me as his next feeding approached. He would come up behind me silently or wait by the door when I left my room, only to disappear after I started from fear.

I would watch for the gradual changes to his face as the time approached. Shadows grew more pronounced under his eyes, and his irises darkened, changing from brilliant red to a muddy burgundy. He stayed handsome but transformed into something more sinister as the day grew closer.

I tried not to lean out into the hallway to look for him when I left my room, but I couldn't help it.

He always caught me in the hall when he fed. He was so fast and quiet that I was always surprised however much I may have been anticipating his attack. Sometimes he leapt out of the library, other times from his office. The scariest times were when he shoved me onto my back on the floor. I was terrified that he might want more than blood on those occasions, but he simply walked away purring when he was done feeding, and Lillian would help me up.

I stayed in my room as much as possible to avoid him until I realized that Mack occasionally left the house.

I would come downstairs alone when I knew he was gone. I didn't want to alienate Lillian by trying to run out the front door when it was just the two of us. She was undoubtedly as strong and fast as Mack. So I would go into the library, select a few books, and take them upstairs to read. Sometimes I imagined that Boo was lying at my feet, sleeping, his warmth soaking through the quilt.

I had gone through their few classics quickly and was making my way through the rest of the collection, desperate to read anything that would distract me. The library contained books on history and religion as well as a variety of titles on real estate, business, and law. There were a lot of books from the 1890s to the 1930s, and complete sets of Encyclopedias with dates beginning in the 1960s and ending with a set published in 2009.

It wasn't only books I was interested in. I was determined to find a way to escape or let someone know I was alive even if I didn't know exactly where I was. I always checked the halls and study for an unattended phone or computer each time I was alone.

But I never saw a landline. They must all have cell phones, I thought glumly. That was going to make it harder to get my hands on a phone.

As the weeks passed, I learned the household routine. Mack had visitors; Lillian did not.

Others that I assumed to be vampires visited but generally without making contact with me.

Generally.

The exception was a tall, rangy man with straight dark hair and a cruel look. He came one afternoon while I was in the kitchen eating lunch.

Mack usually stayed in the kitchen when I was eating lunch and dinner, because he knew I wouldn't eat steak if he wasn't there.

Mack met this guest in the hall by the kitchen door and clapped him on the back.

"Ted," he exclaimed.

It was strange to hear him like this. He sounded carefree and happy as if he was just some average guy.

"Mack," the newcomer said with a laugh.

Ted peered around Mack into the kitchen. From my seat at the table, I could see him looking at me curiously. I scooted my chair closer to Lillian. He gave me an appraising look and smiled the scariest grin I had ever seen.

"Who's this?" he asked Mack.

"She's mine," said Mack sharply before leading him away.

Lillian had slipped into Mack's chair during their exchange, placing herself between me and the visitor in the doorway. I saw a brief smile flash across her face as she looked at Ted and saw him smile back. Mack seemed to watch the exchange with interest and stroked his chin as he looked between them.

I looked at her questioningly when they were gone. "His brother, Ted," she mouthed silently.

I trembled. Would he allow Ted to feed from me?

Lillian sensed my fear—she took my plate and glass and walked me to my room. She sat on the bed and worked on some mending she pulled out of her apron pocket while I finished my lunch.

As I ate I caught a glimpse of myself in the mirror. Though I washed my hair out of habit, it was flat and lackluster, hanging limply on either side of my head. My skin was paler than ever, and I had huge shadows under my eyes.

It occurred to me I was changing into one of them.

"Am I..." I said then paused.

"Are you what?" Lillian asked, guarded.

"I'm getting pale," I said.

"I noticed."

"Am I becoming one of you?"

She put down her mending. "No. That's a process. It can happen accidentally with a younger one who is interrupted during feeding, but Mack is experienced. He won't change you unless he plans to. His venom is stronger since he is older. Traces of it are in your system, left from when he feeds. I can smell it in your scent, but it's not changing you."

"Then what is this?" I asked, gesturing to my face.

"You look miserable," she said flatly.

CHAPTER TWENTY-FOUR

To Kill a Vampire

Though I appeared resigned to my fate, I kept looking for a way to escape or fight.

A few weeks after I arrived, as Lillian and I were preparing lunch one day, Mack waved Lillian out of the kitchen.

"Thought I would eat with her today," he said.

She gave him a dubious look but ducked her head and left when he snarled at her. I cringed at the noise, and he cut his eyes over to me.

Once she was gone, he smiled and went to the refrigerator. He stood in front of the opened French doors as if unfamiliar with the operation of a refrigerator before he poked around inside, pulling out containers and examining the contents. Seeing him like this, I realized that Lillian never turned her back to me in the kitchen. She had been keeping an eye on the knife drawer since the day I arrived.

This was my chance. While Mack was engrossed with the refrigerator, I reached into the unattended cutlery drawer. I pulled out a long, serrated knife I could easily conceal while his back was turned and slid it up my sleeve. Rather than stab him right now, I wanted to prepare.

I kept the knife on me for several days, practicing stabbing someone in the mirror. I found I was surprisingly reluctant to take a swipe at someone. "He isn't alive," I kept telling myself as I thrust it forward, first with both hands, then with only one. What should I aim for? His chest? Hearts, if his did beat, would be protected by the ribcage. His throat? He was taller than I was, so I would have to attack him while he was sitting down. Every move I attempted felt ungainly. I finally decided to go with a stab to the chest.

I had both my nerve and my opportunity a day later when he was sitting next to me during lunch. Something outside had caught his attention, so he was looking into the backyard.

I slid the knife out of my sleeve and thrust it into his chest as hard as I could, jumping to my feet and using my weight as leverage.

To my horror, though the knife slid into his body until stopped by a bone, Mack didn't react to it. My hand slid down the handle when it stopped, and the sharp blade sliced my palm open. I looked down stupidly at my hand then back at him.

In a flash, Mack had the knife handle in one hand and my injured hand in the other. He pulled the knife out of his chest and tossed it on the floor, and then lifted my hand to his mouth as he watched my face intently.

He licked the blood seeping out of the wound slowly and luxuriously as if licking a lollipop. A sharp burning sensation, like I was holding a hot iron, shot through me from where his tongue had touched. I tried to jerk away, but he held my hand steady as he trapped my eyes with his glare.

After a few seconds of staring, he bent back over my hand and sucked at it slightly, then licked my palm and wrist, removing all traces of blood. He then gently turned it back toward me.

The knife cut was now just a small white line.

"Does it still burn?" he asked.

I shook my head, terrified of what he was going to do to me.

"Knives and bullets don't work on us," he stated flatly.

"I wasn't given a manual," I snapped, surprising myself. "What does, then?"

To my surprise, he burst into laughter and ruffled the top of my head while I struggled to free myself from his grasp.

"I'm beginning to like you, little spitfire," he said. "Don't do that again. And if you stab Lillian, Ted will probably kill you the first chance he gets."

He picked up the chair that had tipped over when I attacked him and set me back down on it. Pushing my plate back in front of me, he said, "Now, eat."

CHAPTER TWENTY-FIVE

Looking Out My Window

Nothing changed after I stabbed Mack except that Lillian always accompanied me to the kitchen.

I dreamed of getting away but never found the opportunity.

The season was changing outside my bedroom window. I spent afternoons looking outside at the woods, watching the world. The leaves on the trees at the edge of the property had been changing from green to bright yellows and reds. I had been brought here in August, and it was now mid-September.

I had managed to keep this window for myself. I hadn't tried to climb out—I had seen too many demonstrations of vampire speed and hearing to have any hope of getting far. I wanted this one thing left to me. In the early evenings I watched as darkness grew, first inside the woods just behind the house and then crept across the backyard. I listened to the breeze rustling though the trees and scattering the leaves that had fallen to the ground.

The sounds of the night brought back a sense of normal life. I could close my eyes and imagine I was hearing birds at my grandparents' home in Michigan, not in my current prison. We had often spent summers in their small house outside of Traverse City. The twins, Simon and Simone, would run and yell in the backyard as they played with the dog after we came home from a day at the sand dunes.

One night, as I looked out I saw a shadow on the patio and watched as Mack walked into the backyard. He was moving at human speed and stood still for a moment, his head lifted in the air, eyes closed.

Was he scenting the breeze?

I watched, frozen, as he seemed to change from man to animal and back again.

His eyes shot up to my window, and I pulled back slightly. Then he ran off the patio and into the woods.

I wondered what it was he was tracking. Or whom.

The next morning I had my answer. At breakfast his eyes were bright red, so he must have fed during the night.

I was horrified to realize I felt relief. He had killed someone, or at least fed on someone last night, but that meant that I would be spared my ordeal for a few more days.

CHAPTER TWENTY-SIX

Escape

We had seen a lot of Ted as he had been in town "on business," Lillian told me. He had visited several times in the past week. The rangy vampire seemed to enjoy getting a rise out of me by smirking at me when Mack wasn't looking. To my relief he kept his distance.

One night Lillian came to my room after dinner. She had a starry look in her eyes as she said, "Ted and I will be going away for a few days. Others of my kind will be here but don't worry about them. Just tell Mack if anyone makes you feel uncomfortable."

As if anything could be more "uncomfortable" than being here.

"Have a good time," I told her. I was terrified at the prospect of her absence, but realized that I genuinely wished her happiness. I shook my head at my stupidity. She was one of my captors and a vampire, even if she didn't feed on me. When did she feed? She always seemed to be in the house when I left my room.

Later that night when I woke up, the house was unusually silent. No lights. No sounds.

I got up, pulled on some clothes and crept down the stairs and into the kitchen. I was aware that my captors were naturally very quiet, but no one came out into the hall or into the kitchen as they usually did when they heard me moving about the house.

After a few minutes in the dark, silent kitchen, I still hadn't heard anything. So I opened the back door and stepped outside into the night. There was a full moon overhead with a slight cloud cover.

I was alone in the dark stillness. No one appeared in the doorway to summon me back into the house.

As I walked quietly to the edge of the yard, I held back from sprinting, trying not to make any noise, but started running as soon as I reached the woods behind the house. I pushed through brush that scratched my legs as I passed. Slim branches I never saw whipped back and cut my face, but I kept running, spurred on by the pain—and the sudden fear that Mack might smell the blood.

As I ran, I heard a sniffing sound and a few low growls behind me. I paused a few times to see if I was being pursued. The noises ceased whenever I stopped moving, but as soon as I began running again, the snuffling sounds resumed.

So I continued, stumbling a little and panting, out of shape from the months of inactivity. Finally I came to a stream. The water's surface glistened in the light of the full moon. It didn't look very deep though I couldn't tell for sure.

Water throws off a tracker, right? I hurriedly crossed it on rocks scattered throughout the streambed. Midway across I slipped and fell into the stream, scraping my legs on the sharp stones.

The pain and cold water instantly brought me wide awake and alert, and I no longer worried about being quiet. Once I reached the other bank, I ran headlong, crashing through the brush, tripping every hundred yards, then getting up and running again. Occasionally I would stop to listen for pursuers. The wind had picked up, and the howling sound it made in the trees above was unnerving. I shivered, still wet from the stream.

Finally, I sank to the ground, dead tired. I struggled to listen, to stay awake, but my fear and adrenaline soon gave way to exhaustion.

I awoke with a start. It was growing light above the trees. Day was breaking. I shivered in the cold. My heart was beating fast like something had scared me back to consciousness. I looked around and listened, but I didn't see or hear anyone.

I was surprised no one had found me yet. Maybe they thought I was sleeping? Couldn't they hear me breathe? I didn't know and wasn't going to waste any more time guessing. I needed to move.

I stood up and glanced around, trying to remember which way I had come the night before, but the forest looked the same in all directions. I decided to head in the direction I had been facing when I woke up. Gauging from the sun's position, I was heading west. My window had a west view, so with any luck, I might not have stumbled around in circles all night but been moving steadily further from the house.

I was only wearing ballet flats, not made for cross country treks, and I was beginning to wince with each step. I forced myself on, ignoring my fear of leaving the smell of blood on the ground with each step I took.

CHAPTER TWENTY-SEVEN

Flight

Eventually, I heard the sound of running water again. I didn't know whether to be happy or afraid. Was I back at the stream from the night before?

I finally broke clear of the brush only to see a river in front of me. My heart sank. It was far too wide and fast to swim across. I scrambled down the steep bank to the river's edge. The sight and sound of water made me thirsty, but I knew I shouldn't drink the muddy water.

I walked along the bank. A river this wide needed a bridge, so I was sure to find a road soon. I walked most of the day under the shadow of trees or rocks where possible. Even though it was late October, I could feel the sun burning my pale, exposed skin.

Finally I saw something ahead, glimmering in the sunlight. A white trestle bridge spanned the river.

Hope. Relief. Fear. Emotions battled inside me. If a bridge were this close, I must be near a well-traveled road.

But would Mack or Ted be waiting for me there?

I couldn't afford to think in those terms. Tearing off the bottom of my shirt, I made a bandana that partially shielded my face and trudged forward, exhausted.

Near the bridge, I climbed from the river's edge to higher ground.

The side of the hill was steep, and the tan rocks embedded in the side were loose and tumbled around me with each cautious move I made. A few tree roots emerged among the rocks, probably exposed by a mudslide. I wasn't worried about a mudslide now, I was just glad for the handhold they gave me.

Halfway up the cliff, I felt myself slipping. The root I grabbed pulled loose, and I started sliding down the steep embankment.

As I flailed about, grabbing for anything to prevent this free fall, there was a flash of someone beside me and cold hands grabbed me.

The next moment I was safely on the top of the bank, and Mack was gone.

I stood still, hands on my knees, head bowed, catching my breath. Had he been there all along?

With a sinking heart, I realized that he was playing a game. "He likes to hunt," Lillian had told me.

I sank to the ground, feeling defeated. Every muscle in my body ached. He knew where I was. Why should I continue?

For a moment I just sat, fighting back tears of frustration.

What would happen if I kept going and found someone? Would anyone who tried to help me be killed? That thought gave me pause.

I wouldn't give Mack the satisfaction of returning to the house. I would throw myself off the bridge. That would be my way out.

So I walked toward the bridge, fighting through the brush that grew along the top of the riverbank. The leaves were mostly gone from the trees and bushes, so sharp little branches cut into my legs as I passed. If I tried to push them back, their thorns cut my hands.

Finally I reached a road. When I heard traffic coming, I stepped out onto the shoulder. A large semi slowed down and pulled up next to me. I looked up and saw the driver leaning across the cab to roll down the window. I knew Mack was near, so I was torn as to how to react to this potential Good Samaritan.

"Need a ride, little girl?" the leering truck driver asked.

This guy was not my knight in shining armor.

CHAPTER TWENTY-EIGHT

Return to Captivity

Across the road Mack appeared from behind a cluster of trees. He stood quietly leaning against one of the trunks, making sure I saw him.

He must have been monitoring my every movement, and now he was watching me with this truck driver.

I forced a smile onto my face and looked back at the truck driver. "I'm okay," I said. "Just waiting for my boyfriend to catch up. Who would have guessed I could reach the road from the river bank first?"

The truck driver stared for a moment. "Well, take this hat," he said, tossing a large-brimmed work hat at me. "You must have been out there for quite a while; I don't see many sunburns this time of year. Not too late to reconsider…" he said as he motioned to the seat in the cab next to him.

I caught the hat and shook my head. He was a nice man; I wouldn't risk getting him killed. "Thanks, Mister. Mine blew into the river."

He nodded, shifted into gear, and pulled away, leaving me standing alone at the side of the road. My choice.

"What's the plan?" I said, knowing Mack could hear me.

Silence.

I was tired and worn out. I wanted my ordeal over, but I couldn't put another human in danger as well. It only took a few seconds to decide. If I lived, I would continue to be slowly drained by this vampire until either he tired of me or lost control during one of his feedings. If I wanted to die on my terms, this was my chance. On shaky legs, I made my way into the center of the left lane and sat down where an oncoming truck would hit me.

I closed my eyes as I heard the sound of a diesel engine. The truck was approaching fast—with any luck, he wouldn't see me. I heard an ear-shattering honk and the screech of brakes.

Before it could hit me, I was lifted and carried by strong, cold arms. I gave in to the fear, exhaustion, and pain, and began sobbing. He held me and ran as I cried.

In a short time, we were back in the house. Mack placed me in the middle of my bed.

"Enjoy your jaunt?" he said, pacing in front of me. "I take it I have to lock you up now?"

I stared at him then closed my eyes and fell back without answering. I dropped off immediately into the sleep of exhaustion.

When I woke up in the morning, I moaned. Every muscle in my body ached. I put my hands gingerly on my face, testing for the sunburn I had felt yesterday.

To my surprise, it didn't hurt. Running my hands down my legs, which had been covered with tiny cuts from where branches had sliced into them as I ran, I saw they were now scratch-free. As I reached my feet, I could see white marks where the blisters had been, but they were no longer painful.

A movement in the corner of the room stopped my examination. Mack was sitting in the rocking chair, legs crossed, a stony expression on his face. When I looked at him, he caught my eyes with his and held my gaze. I quickly lost the staredown, dropped my glance to the floor, and pulled my legs under me. I pushed back a feeling of shame that flashed through me. *Why am I ashamed? Because I failed to escape? Or because I disappointed him?*

He got up and handed me two large bottles of clear fluid. "Drink these," he ordered. "You need to replenish your electrolytes. I'll need to feed tomorrow, so you need to drink. If you don't, I'll have them put in via an I.V."

I made a face as I gulped down the Gatorade. It tasted nasty. I hated him.

But I paused between gulps.

"Why?" I asked.

He stared at me without answering.

"Why me?"

He sat down in the chair again and leaned back, crossing one leg atop the other. "Because I wanted you," he replied.

A smile crept across his face. I shivered.

CHAPTER TWENTY-NINE

Discouraging Conversations

"Why wait until I was coming home from Italy?" I asked Mack. "Why not Chicago?"

"That was because of Mr. Amalfi," Mack replied. "He told me I couldn't take you in Chicago since you were the daughter of a woman connected to a politician. But when you snapped his picture in the airport, it raised the threat of exposure...which meant you were all mine," he said simply.

"Millicent?" I asked softly.

He raised an eyebrow.

"Millicent Berrywhite, the attorney I worked for at the law firm," I said more forcefully. "Did you kill her?"

He shook his head. "No, I didn't. She might have preferred it, though. She's at the facility Duane took you to originally. She'll live there until she is no longer of any use to us."

So my suspicions about the ranch-style buildings being holding cells were correct. I was horrified at the thought of the brilliant Millicent being kept there but tried not to let my feelings show. Since I was getting answers from him for the first time, I decided to keep pushing.

"Why?" I asked.

"Why?" he repeated.

"What had Millicent done?"

"She was too nosy, investigating things that were none of her business," he said flatly, signaling an end to the conversation.

My heart sank, and I shivered. I had been so close to her. She may have spent three days in the same room I had with Betty bringing her food.

With nothing else to ask, I continued downing the Gatorade. When I was done, he left me alone. I spent the rest of the day looking out the window as I reconsidered my escape options. Maybe if I could get one of the cars...but he knew who my mother was. Even If I got away, I could never go home. As I stared outside, feeling hope leave me.

When I saw Lillian at dinner that night, she kept a straight face. Not stern, just straight. It was steak for dinner, of course, and extra rare. Even with Mack there,

I was choking on the texture of the nearly raw meat. When I finished eating, Mack left the room.

Finally, Lillian spoke. "We both suffered from that, you know," she said softly. "My wounds are healed, the same as yours."

"How—and why did he hurt you?" I asked. "You weren't even here."

"First, the how," she said as she washed the frying pan. "Our saliva has healing properties. As long as it's on the surface, it won't change you. That's how your cuts were healed, just like with the knife wound to your hand."

She turned to look at me. "And why? I knew you were going to make a run for it."

I started to say something, and she shook her head, smiling affectionately. "No way you wouldn't. You have spunk—you're like me. I told him you would run. I guess he thinks I didn't try hard enough to convince him."

"I'm sorry," I said, and I was. She was the closest thing I'd had to a companion during this ordeal. Not warm, but reliable.

"Don't worry," she stated. "He enjoyed his little hunt. I'm sure he wished it had lasted longer."

"I needed the exercise," I said. "I hadn't realized how out of shape I am. Spending that time on the run made me realize I need to get on a treadmill or something. Hit the gym more regularly."

I saw a small smile flash across her face, but she quickly hid it.

"Am I going to die?" I asked in a small voice.

"All the rest of us are dead, honey," said Lillian matter-of-factly.

CHAPTER THIRTY

Lillian's Life and Times

I stared at her. "How did you get here? Is that what happened to you?"

She paused and appeared to consider her answer before replying.

"Mack didn't change me," she said. "I was born in Oklahoma. I was a teenager during the Dust Bowl. After two years of crop failures, my family began talking about heading for California, but I didn't want to go. I had a sweetheart in town, and I believed my future lay with him." She smiled ruefully, rocking on her feet.

"At least, I thought he was my sweetheart," she continued. "Turns out I was just another girl to him. And he had lots of us.

When my folks packed up the truck to leave, I snuck off. I had to walk all night to get into town and hid in roadside ditches whenever I heard trucks passing by. My father drove by twice, but I ducked out of sight each time.

I remember in the morning, just before I got to town, watching the storm coming in. It looked like a big, black cloud rolling in. You couldn't keep the dust out of the house. During the storms that had come before, we tried hanging wet sheets, but nothing worked. Cattle died with two inches of dirt in their stomach. You ever see a sand storm when you were at the picture show?"

I realized she meant movies. "Yes," I replied. "I saw *Lawrence of* Arabia and *The Mummy*. They both had sand storms."

"Well, dust storms could stretch across states," she told me. "Some were so big they looked like clouds on the ground. Billowing, black clouds that brought death."

She sat down and her eyes grew unfocused as she appeared to become lost in her memories.

I tried to recall what I knew about the Dust Bowl. "So, your family had a farm?"

"We were famers, but we didn't own the land, so we were forced to leave. I went home after two weeks and found a note from my father tied to a tree by the front door. They couldn't wait any longer. Told me to join up with someone else and meet them in California. My mother wrote at the bottom of the note that she hoped I had gotten married and would send her pictures of my children.

I walked east instead of west though. Looking back, that time must have been easy for my kind. So many people were just unaccounted for. I was adrift as I looked for work of any kind in Oklahoma City. As a pretty girl I got offers, but most weren't for respectable work. I worked in motels and restaurants, mostly."

"What happened to your boyfriend?" I asked. "Couldn't he help?"

She stared at me. "Married," she said.

"Sorry," I replied reflexively.

She shrugged. "One night on my way back to the room I was renting, I sensed I was being followed. By that time, I was used to men tailing me, and I carried a gun in my purse.

I pulled it out and pointed it at him when he closed in. But he shoved me against the wall and grabbed the gun from me before I could pull the trigger. He bit me, but instead of killing me decided to keep me as company. I was never happy, and eventually we separated."

"What was it like?" I asked.

"What was what like?" she said.

"Becoming a vampire. Did it hurt?"

She looked at me and seemed to weigh her words carefully. "You die. You can feel your body die, but you don't lose consciousness. You wait for it to end, pray for it to be over, but it doesn't end. Slowly you lose control of your extremities, and then all feeling leaves. You're trapped inside of a corpse-body. It's not a good feeling and seems to last forever. You're suspended. I thought I was in Limbo, and God was punishing me for my affair with a married man and abandoning my family.

Maybe He was, and maybe I still am.

But eventually that phase ends, and when you can move again, you burn with a terrible thirst."

"Sounds awful," I said.

She nodded. "One night I wandered into an all-night revival meeting in Mack's territory. These were very popular at the time. People came from all over to attend, so a strange woman wouldn't be noticed as women were common at revival meetings. I often found my victims outside the tents.

I was circling the crowd, looking for a loner to lure away, when I caught sight of Mack. I saw him flick his eyes my way, and I tried to run."

She paused and pulled her arms to her chest, hugging herself.

"You've seen him as a human sees a vampire," she said. "You know how scary he is to you as a mortal. What you don't know is how intimidating he is to others of my kind."

She rocked herself slightly in the chair.

"I was terrified of him. He caught up to me quickly, and I stopped. I was beat down, because I didn't have a place to go. He circled me several times, but I held my head down and didn't put up a fight. When he asked where I was from, I told him nowhere.

Mack stopped circling and stood in front of me while I waited for the death blow. You don't poach on another vampire's territory. Even though I didn't know it was claimed, by all rights, he could have just destroyed me.

But he didn't. Instead, he brought me to this house, and I've been here ever since. That's all there is about me. I stay here. He leaves and comes back.

Funny, he gave me all I wanted. A home."

She rocked some more and tucked a lock of hair behind her ear. I could almost see her as a human, sitting on her front porch, watching the dust cloud coming.

"What about Mack?" I asked her.

"What about him?" she said brusquely.

"How was he changed?"

"I don't know all the details. He's from around here—that I do know. He was changed during the 1930s, after Prohibition ended. Ran a still while he was alive, probably more than one, during the Depression. He was tough when he was living, a man not to be messed with. He's still the same way."

She had given me a lot to think about. We sat in silence for a few minutes, and then I went upstairs to my room.

CHAPTER THIRTY-ONE

Trouble Brewing

It was now almost Christmas. I had been in Europe in August, so I could only imagine how frantic my family must feel not to have heard from me.

Mack had mentioned knowing my mother had political connections. This combined with his comment about the threat of exposure made me wonder whether my family was in danger. I feared not just for myself and my parents but for my friends.

My worries became focused when Mack's next visitors came.

I was standing in the library doorway when they arrived. Mack met the antiquities dealer, Mr. Amalfi, at the front door. As Mack greeted him, I saw Mr. Amalfi looking my way. When our eyes met, I saw sadness flash across his face, but it was quickly gone. Mack followed his gaze, and I shrank back. I went into the kitchen just as a second vampire entered the kitchen from the garage. I froze when I saw him, my heart pounding. It was the vampire who grabbed me at the airport, Duane.

When Duane saw me, he looked at me hungrily. I backed out of the kitchen and into the hallway, and immediately Mack was standing next to me. I heard them hissing, and Mack's stare went flat. Mack surprised me by putting his arm around my waist and pulling me to his side as he turned my face into his chest. I involuntarily reached up and took hold of his shirt, then let go when I realized what I had done.

Lillian appeared, pulled me back into the library, and sat down with her knitting.

"We're just going to stay in here for a while," she said. "They'll be leaving soon."

"What's going on out there?" I asked.

"Duane is Mr. Amalfi's driver," Lillian said in a low voice. "He thinks you should be his as he was the one who took the risk when he snatched you from the crowded airport. The only question is whether he's foolish enough to challenge Mack."

"Challenge him?" I asked.

"There are rules in our world," she explained. "Actually, only one. No, make that two. First, humans can't know about us. Second, when it comes to vampire fights, if you survive, you've won. And the winner takes all. That's how vampires acquire wealth and territory."

I thought for a few seconds, remembering the time Mack and Duane had fought in the hallway. "They'll fight over me again?" I finally asked. "Why?"

"You smell good to us. Young women always smell good to us, but the scent of your fear is particularly tantalizing," Lillian stated simply. "You're young, so you'll probably last a while."

My heart sank.

"The last time I saw Duane, Mack ripped off his arm," I said. "Yet today, it looked like he had both arms again. How?"

"We can heal ourselves using our saliva. You saw a small example of this ability when Mack healed the cuts you sustained in your run through the woods. You have to burn our bodies to truly end our immortality. Losing a limb hurts, but it can be healed. When we want to kill another of our kind, we tear off the head. That can't be healed easily. It takes someone skilled in the art of healing our kind—and arriving on the scene soon after the dismemberment—to make it work at all. If not, you don't even need to burn the body. Just leave it there."

I considered this new bit of information in silence for a few seconds before she continued.

"Mack hasn't been that bad to you, overall," she said. "He doesn't want to deal with a suicidal human or one who has to be under lock and key. I've been places where humans were treated far worse, just so you know."

"I ran once," I said, ticking off the list of my trans-gressions on my fingers, "and I stabbed him."

She smiled. "Yeah, honey, you sure did."

CHAPTER THIRTY-TWO

So It Was Montana

"How long have the others lasted?" I asked Lillian.

She looked at me, puzzled. "Others?"

"The other people, before me," I replied.

"There were no others," she stated. "He prefers to hunt. We all do, quite frankly."

"Then why me?"

"Mack told me that if he had found you while out hunting, he would have killed you," she said in a chillingly matter-of-fact voice. "But you were in Chicago, Mr. Amalfi's territory. He picked up your scent while he was on surveillance, so he put in a claim. Mack was there because Mr. Amalfi asked him to look into an investigation someone was doing. He felt the human was getting close to discovering our identities.

Mr. Amalfi declined Mack's initial request as your disappearance would attract too much attention. You were a student with a future; your mother worked for a powerful politician."

"Why would Mack be doing work for Mr. Amalfi?" I asked.

"Mr. Amalfi is Mack's sire. He found Mack in St. Louis in the 1930s when Mack brought his liquor into town to sell. Mr. Amalfi needed someone to help with his security, and he liked how Mack handled himself. Mack lived with him for a while, but within a few years, he wanted to come back here. They parted amicably; occasionally he still helps Mr. Amalfi with security matters. I met him shortly after he returned."

"They took Millicent," I said.

"Who's that?" Lillian asked.

"My boss from Chicago," I replied. "That's who he was doing the surveillance on."

"Don't know about that," Lillian replied. "But once you had been brought into our world, he claimed you in Montana."

"That's where I was?" I said, shuddering, remembering the plane ride and the terrifying house in the middle of nowhere.

"Yep. That's one of the places we keep humans. They live out their lives on ranches or similar locations, and a doctor draws their blood on a regular basis. The blood gets bottled and sold much the way humans bottle and sell beer. We even use similar bottles and bottling techniques. That way we don't have to hunt if we don't want to."

"That's where Moltadano is," I said.

Lillian started. "How do you know about Moltadano?"

"I read about him in a book. Then I saw him at that house in Montana."

Lillian relaxed a little, shaking her head. "Moltadano is one of the oldest among us. I don't think he has visited the United States. He stays in France, and just like Amalfi has Duane and used to have Mack, he has men who go out for him."

She looked perplexed. "I'm surprised he let a book naming him exist."

"The man who was selling it is...gone now. He was hiding it in his bookstore. I think he hoped anyone searching would look in his house, not his shop."

She nodded.

"Who was the man at the house in Montana, then?" I asked.

"Oh, he was just a business man. I think his name is Randolph. Runs his business like a brewery with similar issues of bottling, distributing."

"How many?" I asked.

"How many what?" she said.

"How many of us do you guys have?"

"No idea," she said, and then picked up her knitting. It was the end of our conversation. Apparently I had brought up things she wasn't supposed to discuss.

A few hours later, I heard the visitors leave and went back to my room. I lay down on my bed, trying to get my head around this world I had been caught up in. What had Millicent found in Chicago? Whatever it was, it cost us both our freedom.

She had tried so hard to keep me safe by sending me on what I thought was my dream trip to France—attempting to get me far enough away that I wouldn't be caught.

I had blown it by snooping around and taking Mr. Amalfi's photo. But then I wouldn't be me if I hadn't tried to find her.

CHAPTER THIRTY-THREE

Duane Returns

One night I was in my room when I heard the black car pull away from the house with Mack in it. I immediately relaxed, feeling the tension leaving my body. When he was gone, it felt simpler to breathe.

A few minutes later, though, my peace was interrupted. The car was coming back.

But something wasn't right. I was used to hearing the car pull up the driveway and slide into the garage which opened automatically. Tonight, the car stopped before entering the garage.

I pulled on a robe, left my room, and went to the top of the stairs.

I saw Lillian standing at the foot of the steps by the front door. She looked up at me with a worried expression. "It isn't them. Go back to your room and keep the door closed," she whispered as she pulled out her phone and punched in numbers.

A chill ran down my spine. I closed my door and sat on my bed, listening to the sound of her voice below though I couldn't make out the words.

There was a knock at the front door, followed by a few seconds of silence. Then I heard a loud crash followed by a bang. Someone must have kicked open the front door. I heard a low exchange and then a strange sound like stone being crushed. I recalled it instantly. It was the sound I heard when Mack had torn off Duane's arm.

I raced to my door, yanked it opened, and looked down over the bannister to see two men in the hallway with Lillian. One was tearing off her head—he tossed it on the floor just as I got to the railing. The other, who turned to look up at me, was only too familiar.

It was Duane. He was standing next to the front door which was lying on the floor in the hallway, ripped from its hinges. Our eyes met, and his face twisted in a sadistic smile, his red eyes glowing with delight.

I gasped and froze, too terrified to move. Several things happened at the same time, and it seemed like they were in slow motion though I knew they must be occurring at incredible speed.

The strange vampire flicked on a cigarette lighter and dropped it on Lillian's body, catching her dress on fire. At the same time, I heard a car screech to a halt in front of the house and footsteps outside skidding on the gravel.

Meanwhile I was knocked off my feet. Duane had run up the stairs so fast I didn't see him. He grabbed me around the waist and clutched me to his chest as he leapt over the bannister to the first floor then bolted toward the back of the house. We were in motion before I could even register that he had moved.

He smashed through the back door with one shoulder. I felt pain explode around me as my shoulder was slammed into the broken doorframe. I opened my mouth to scream but he put his free hand over my mouth.

"Shut it," he hissed at me.

Something told me he wasn't worried about my shoulder.

Within seconds we were heading into the darkened woods behind the house, Duane running full out. The only light was from a quarter moon overhead which barely broke through the shadows of the trees. Duane didn't just run along the ground though. He leapt from tree to boulder as he plunged deeper into the forest. His grip was so tight that I couldn't breathe. I struggled to catch my breath, tugging at his hand, but to no avail. He wasn't looking at me but was focused on what lay in front of him.

Eventually, he loosened his grip slightly so I could breathe. He must have run for miles. I looked behind me but couldn't see in the darkness, so I listened for any signs of a pursuer. I couldn't hear anything other than Duane's footsteps. Finally, I heard a familiar sound ahead of us. It was the sound of running water.

I turned my head to look in front of us and saw that we were at the river—the one I remembered from my escape attempt.

Duane set me down under a huge pine tree, and I took a deep breath. But I only had a second of respite. Shoving me against the rough pine, he pushed up my chin with one hand, ducking his head for a better angle, and bit my throat, tearing at it savagely.

I shrieked in pain.

He cursed again and clamped his hand back over my mouth. He clutched the back of my neck with his other hand, holding me up using his body, and sucked greedily at my neck.

I felt myself growing weaker with each draw of blood he took. Everything was going black around me. I kept shoving at him, pushing him back, but was losing strength by the second. I was vaguely aware of being lifted and then flung through the air. I'm a bird or an angel, I thought, sure that I was dying.

The River

The sensation of flying didn't last. I hit the river with a splashing thud. The impact brought me back to full consciousness, and I struggled against the shock of cold water flooding into my mouth and lungs. I couldn't breathe and realized that I had survived being bitten only to face death by drowning.

It will soon be over.

But I wasn't quite ready to let go of life, so I fought for air. Each second was agonizing, yet I kept going. I began to wonder how long it takes to drown as I fought to cough out water, only to draw in more with my next inhalation. Soon I realized something was competing for control of my body with the water in my lungs. I could feel my outer extremities growing cold as life left them.

Finally I lay still in the water, unable to breathe, yet unable to die. I was floating, probably near the bottom. I could see water above me and was aware of movement around me as fish and other animals slid over my body. I felt their small nibbles at my mouth and hands, but there was nothing I could do except blink my eyes in an effort to protect them.

The cold that had begun in my hands and feet was steadily creeping across my body. It seemed to be winning the fight against the water in my lungs to claim me. I was in agony. *Please just let it end.*

But it wouldn't. The suffocation continued. I watched the slow progress of the sun above the surface of the water. It had passed over completely and been replaced with darkness. I had no strength to fight my way to the surface or do anything but stare dully overhead as I blinked to keep away the fish that wanted to nibble at my eyes.

The crush of the suffocation stopped. The fight inside was over. There was no more struggle—no more noise inside of my body, neither breathing nor a beating heart. I was suspended between two worlds, just as I was suspended in the water between the air and ground. I don't know how long I remained like this. It seemed an eternity. Lillian's chilling words came back to me, and I had the same thought: Had God rejected me?

A fish nibbled at my finger, and I flicked it away. Realizing I could move, I bent forward at the waist and discovered I was free of the paralysis that had kept me at the bottom of the river.

I quickly pushed myself out the river. As I burst into the air, I thrashed and flung water, rocks, and mud in all directions. When I fell back into the water, I pushed back black handfuls as I fought my way to the shore. Finally I felt ground under my feet, and I used my legs and hands to climb onto the riverbank. I was on solid ground, kneeling on all fours in the mud but free of my watery prison.

I cleared my lungs by spitting out water. It took a few minutes before I realized that I didn't need to breathe. That could only mean I was dead.

I glanced down and saw my reflection.

I was now one of them. A vampire.

I had red eyes. My hair clung to my skull, and my face looked different. The last time I saw my reflection, I had bags under my eyes and appeared listless. Now that I was dead, my face had sharpened into something strange and beautiful. My eyes were luminous, despite being red. The brows that arched above my eyes framed them to perfection. My nose was smoother and more elegant, and my pale complexion flawless. My cheekbones had hollows that any screen actress would envy. I had become an alluring predator.

And I was totally alone.

I leapt up and ran, confused, fleeing from myself and what I had become. To my surprise I was moving fast, very fast, just skimming the surface of the ground.

I had never been athletic and was used to tiring quickly. My escape attempt popped into my memory then vanished. Now, my speed was amazing. I didn't tire, and my feet barely touched the ground. For a fleeting second, it was exhilarating.

My feelings quickly turned to horror. Was I now like Mack? Doomed to feeding on the living? And worse, what would Mack do when he found me? My thoughts were jumbled; I vaguely remembered someone telling me that Mack was terrifying to other vampires.

I ran all night, wanting to leave the confusion behind, not caring where I was going as long as it was away from where I had been. I moved silently between the tall, black trees silhouetted sharply in the moonlight above. Occasionally I jumped over ribbons of concrete that must have been roads, and sometimes I ran through rivers.

As the sun came up an amazing smell caught my attention, and my body felt a hunger it had never experienced before. I turned in the direction of the scent, sniffing the air as I got closer, sensing a heartbeat and warmth ahead of me. Once I was within range, I pounced on the lone creature whose scent had called to me and ripped into the soft body that yielded so easily. After I yanked the head back with my hands for better access to the throat, the body stopped struggling. As I tore into the neck, the blood poured out easily into my mouth, satisfying and quenching my hunger. Finally, there was no more blood, and I stopped, satisfied and sated in a way I had never felt. I closed my eyes, leaned back, and lifted my face to the sky as I luxuriated in this new feeling.

The glow didn't last. When I looked down, I was holding the body of a man. His throat was torn out, and his eyes were bulging. His blood covered his body, the ground, and me. I threw the corpse away from me as soon as I realized what it was, springing back in horror.

But I couldn't run from what I had done. I sat on my haunches and stared across the clearing at the mangled body. I had killed a man. But he had tasted so good, and I had been so hungry.

I approached the body again and realized he had been a fisherman. He wore a fisherman's vest; a fishing pole and other sporting equipment were nearby. He looked young, maybe mid-twenties. Brown hair, medium height, and a simple gold band on his left hand. This fisherman had somebody's husband, maybe even a father. He was a son, friend, colleague...and I had just ended all that.

I agonized—sobbing as I knelt next to him, rocking back and forth. Whether my grief was for him or myself I didn't know.

I realized that I was truly alone. I couldn't go back to my family or friends as I would be a threat to them. I needed to keep going, get far away from here. My sense was that bad things would happen to them if I went back even if I could control my blood craving.

Finally I weighted the fisherman's body with some of his gear and a rock and tossed him into the fast-moving river, watching the body sink into the dark water. I couldn't help but think that just a few hours before, I had been beneath the surface of another river. But this body was dead. I had seen that in his eyes and the way his head lolled loosely on his broken neck. I sent the rest of his fishing equipment into the water after him to keep him company and took off running again. Running without a sense of a destination, only knowing I was heading south.

I only stopped when the scent of prey got to me. At first, I would swerve and speed up to outrun its allure. But the longer I avoided it, the bigger the bloodbath when I gave in. And I always gave in.

After a while I gave up fighting my instinct to kill and just fed.

CHAPTER THIRTY-FIVE

Southbound

Slowly, as I traveled, I began to regain myself. The jumble of senses that had filled my early days in a stream of light, speed, and the scent of food gave way to memories and rational thought. I forced myself to remember who I was.

It took a while to remember my name. The names of those I was fleeing, Mack and Duane, had come to me immediately. My own name, however, did not. Finally, I forced my thoughts to circle down from fear and flight to recall my identity.

I was Christa. Christa…the last name stayed tantalizingly out of reach. Images of my mother, brother and sister flashed across my mind amid flashes of childhood scenes and places I had lived. I tried to focus, but they kept slipping away, giving way to other images and visions of water and sky. Floating on water and laughing. I

165

was in a sailboat looking up at clouds and birds. Then images of beautiful, elegant cities. All of these must have been scenes from my life, but none would stay long enough for me to assemble a coherent story of who I had been.

Finally, I could focus enough to read. I saw a newspaper lying on the side of the road. I picked it up, feeling the texture of the paper in my hands. Memories flashed through me from contact with the newsprint. Images of sitting at a table, laughing with someone as I read a story aloud. I snapped my teeth in anger as the memory slipped out of reach after flitting so close to bringing back meaningful moments from my former life. I shook my head. It wasn't the past I needed to know about, it was the present.

Read. Yes, I could read. Reading used to create a meaningful link to past worlds. Now, it gave me a chance to leave the haze I had existed in and see what I had missed. I looked down at the newsprint in my hands. I noticed that the paper had a scent. It had an acrid smell, possibly from the ink. There was a slight scent of mold as the paper had been lying on the wet ground. Scent now overrode most of my senses, but I struggled to focus on sight in order to read. I saw photos, pictures of an airplane that was lying on the ground next to an image of a stern-looking man in a uniform. I couldn't read the headlines. I recognized the letters but they weren't forming words. Frustrated, I growled. Finally I realized that the headlines were in another language, something that looked like Spanish but wasn't. Portuguese, maybe? I could guess at the date, though, and it appeared months had passed.

I tossed the paper onto the ground and pressed forward.

Time wasn't relevant to me; my only marker for its passage was my recurring hunger. I must have been running for a long time since I was deep in a jungle. I only left it when I needed to feed.

I came across cities as I ran and learned that many of them had small shanty towns outside the metropolis where people crammed into small spaces. The odor was both fragrant from their human blood and rank from the raw sewage. The structures of tin and cardboard were flimsy as I discovered when I jumped atop one while hunting.

The density of the population meant that I couldn't grab just one person. I had to take an entire family if I took one. I hunted along the outskirts of these cities and then withdrew back into the jungle to continue my run south.

There were many rivers and streams in this landscape I was crossing, and sometimes I found people along them. If I found a river when I was hungry, I would run east until I located prey. If necessary I fed on a small pig or jaguar to tide me over until I could find a human.

Time passed. How much? Weeks? Months? The days had gotten both longer and shorter in succession. How long had I been running? It must have been months as it was now spring in this southern world.

Wherever I was now, there was a war going on. I found stacks of bodies, mangled corpses of people who had been shot or bludgeoned to death. Some corpses were fresh. Some wore military uniforms and others appeared to be civilians, often women clutching children.

The sight of the dead women always sent me into a frenzy, and it was never hard to track down their killers. I would climb as high as I could into the tree canopy while following their scents, then drop down and kill them when I located them. I left these new bodies I created on top of the piles that I found, a fitting monument to their handiwork. They were now as discarded as their victims, left to rot without proper burial.

I now had a sense of purpose—I was an avenging angel of sorts. I had found a place, however grim, in the world.

The small armies moving through the jungles meant plenty of food without guilt because as far as I could tell, the guerrilla soldiers would be dead soon whether I was here or not. Without planning to, I lingered.

These men with guns traveled in groups, and I followed them easily from the tops of trees above their heads. Occasionally, one of the men on the ground seemed to sense me, and he would spur the others to move quickly. But they were never quick enough to escape me. I could pick off the last man in a line or wait until they were asleep.

One day I caught sight of my bloody reflection in the river, and I was shocked. My hair was caked with mud, and my eyes looked demonic, wild and red. I now understood the look of terror in the eyes of the men I hunted when they saw me.

Who was I? Had I become like these jungle armies only immortal? How could I escape this existence? Despairing, I sank to my knees and looked around me. Beauty was everywhere in the trees and animals, flashing past me in bursts of color from the birds. I was a blight, an unnatural, unholy thing ruining this paradise.

I decided I would stay in the jungle within the shelter of the trees. I didn't need to make any more nighttime forays to the edges of cities as the war gave me plenty to eat. I continued to watch the brightly colored birds fly by, and I saw huge snakes catching animals that looked like small pigs.

I could feel my mind slipping away.

CHAPTER THIRTY-SIX

Blood Demon

I noticed a change in my prey's behavior.

The groups I hunted huddled close together, and they were always armed. They never slept at the same time, as one always stayed awake to stand guard. I listened from my treetop perch as I waited for them to go to sleep before I attacked. Occasionally they spoke in Spanish, and I heard stories of a demon in the jungle. A fierce thing—a woman with wild hair, spattered in blood, who appeared from nowhere.

With a shock, I realized it was me. Not only did I consider myself a monster, but the humans around me had recognized this truth. I was a blood demon to them.

I fled the scene, racing through the treetops to get away. As I ran my thinking continued to alter and slant. Things stopped making sense, and try as I might to focus, only one thing mattered.

I was a blood demon.

How could I expiate this? How could I exorcise what I had become?

I raised my reddened hands to the sky, my offering to the Sun above, if only He would stop the burning in my throat.

Everything circled and raced inside my head.

I ran, seeking to clear my mind, but the clamor and the noise wouldn't stop. The looks of terror and last cries of my victims haunted me. These horrific sights and sounds drowned out the world around me, circling in endless loops in my head, continually building up into a crescendo that I couldn't stand.

I was forced to stop running and knelt with one hand on either side of my head. If I could push the noise out of my head by pressing on my ears I would, but that didn't work. I hadn't felt this much internal pain and chaos since I lay on the bottom of the river, however long ago that had been. If that had even ever happened— I was no longer sure of anything.

Finally it was silent inside.

Exhausted, I opened my eyes and slowly stood up.

The world slanted, and I swayed. The chaos calmed, and I felt surrounded by walls of blinding light, encircling me. When I looked up, I saw the light's messengers, angels, all around me, circling overhead. Some were dark, others were light. As I gazed around, I realized the Sun's messengers had been with me all along in those bright flashes of color in the jungle. Angels. Bird wings. Messengers. Butterflies.

If I could fly, I would be free. Free of the thirst. Free of the blood that has drenched through to my soul.

I wanted to fly. I reached up to the Sun, begging Him to take me.

But the Sun went away, and I was cast into night. He would reappear again on the opposite side of the sky in the morning, and I watched and waited through the dark hours for His return. Slowly, the sky began to glow red, signaling the Sun's coming. Soon He was overhead, a blinding white ball, swirling out His energy in waves of purifying rays.

I raised my hands above my head, stretching. I felt the sensation of light falling in sheets around me, on all sides. I put my head back, closing my eyes, showing that I was ready to be taken up into its purifying fire away from the bloody earth.

But the Sun never granted me freedom from the ground. He left me standing and sank into the ground at night. In the morning, He returned.

My offerings were not enough. What would satisfy Him? I kept running south, staying clear of the temptation of the living in an effort to purify myself though that meant fighting the maddening thirst. I stayed deep inside the trees to avoid those thrumming heartbeats signaling food nearby.

After a time I heard someone behind me. I had been the pursuer, but now I was the pursued. I realized that whoever was behind me had no heartbeat.

A prickling at the back of my neck said it was another demon, or perhaps two.

I dropped to the ground from the treetops I had made my home and snapped my head around, searching for my pursuers.

I sensed they were close.

I hadn't been on the ground for a long time; I'd stayed at the tops of trees. I pulled one leg up so that my foot rested on the other knee, tipping my head back to scent the breeze. I pulled both arms above me in a v with fingers pointed down. Could I fly this time? I closed my eyes, hoping the Sun would hear my prayer and be ready to receive me. I waited, sure that He would grant me wings.

I swayed. No response. My body was still the same.

But in the time I had spent on the ground, the danger had come closer. The sound of the breeze brought the murmur of voices though I couldn't understand the words. I closed my eyes to focus on the soft sounds of my pursuers. Tilting my head forward, facing the trees in front of me, I could hear them approaching. I opened my eyes to see—across a clearing—a glimpse of long brown hair and a shoulder that quickly vanished back into the trees. I was now the hunted.

I inhaled a musty male scent and found longings awakening that I hadn't experienced around human men. Strange, strong feelings, coupled with a desire to be with others of my kind.

I fought the feelings, pushing them back. No. I was a demon, and this was the enemy approaching.

Instinctively I tipped my head forward so I was looking down and lowered both arms toward the ground, as if in defeat and submission, but kept my eyes open in tiny slits.

The sounds of their voices resolved themselves into words, but they meant nothing to me.

Two demons with brown hair appeared. They separated at the edge of the clearing, and one walked directly toward me while the other circled the perimeter just inside the tree cover.

Did they think I couldn't see them?

I tested my arms and found that I had not been granted wings, so I bolted. I felt my insides fighting me, yearning to be with one of them, but I pushed back those feelings. I was a demon but had been seeking sanctuary from my evil. In time I was sure that Sun would purify me if I could prove that I wanted expiation enough.

I took to the treetops, moving easily in the familiar world of the overhead branches. I knew which ones would hold my weight, and I heard the two men falling behind, dropping from the trees as they tried to follow. They called after me, a name that tugged on the edges of my awareness and almost made me pause: "Christa."

No. I wouldn't answer.

I kept going away, always in the same direction. Noon rays at my back, morning rays to my left. Only the exertion of keeping my legs moving had meaning.

Gradually, I noticed that the trees thinning and rocks taking over the landscape. There were no sounds other than the wind along this rocky wasteland. Soon only water was along one side of my path, and I heard birds over the ocean.

Finally there was nothing but water. I ran along the edge of the land, but there was no more land unless I turned north.

I had come to the end of the world.

CHAPTER THIRTY-SEVEN

Starvation

I sat down. I could see a few small islands in the distance, but the circling birds were my only living companions.

I continued to make my appeals to Sun to change me, to take me up into the air to be one of His winged angels. I stood on the boulders that bordered the ocean and waited, head tilted back so my face was bathed in warm rays, eyes closed, arms above me in a v, hoping that this time He would choose to free me from this existence.

I stopped eating, hoping to purify myself of the blood I had stolen from the living. I may not have chosen this life, but I could choose what I did within the confines of it. The thought that by denying myself the blood of any living creature I could end the burden of my existence gave me hope. The pain of the thirst was constant, but I hoped its fire would either contribute to my purification or end me altogether.

I longed to be free of this existence.

But I was still weak. Sometimes my hunger made me leap for the birds and occasionally I caught one. The tiny amount of blood I drained from their broken bodies meant that I stayed alive a bit longer, but it also undoubtedly made Sun unwilling to lift me up.

I liked the birds' feathers though. I made myself wings from these feathers to show Sun my dreams. I created a large design with feathers of varying sizes and shapes. The wings were twice my length, and the feathers arranged in patterns of ripples, like the waves of the sea that surrounded three-quarters of my rocky promontory. The shades of gray and white undulated in curves that would start at my shoulder and extend to twice the length of my arms, ready to carry me far from this place. I kept them safe from the wind in a small cave created by a depression in the rocks.

I hoped this offering might help appease Sun for the death of His winged messengers. If He accepted it, perhaps He would let me shed the burden of this thirst-ridden body, and I would be able to fly up into the sky.

More time passed. I couldn't see much—everything was slowing down. Gray above me, gray all around. I could feel my body shutting down. Instead of standing, I lay on the rock closest to the water facing the sky. Sun continued his circle above me as time crept past.

It shouldn't be much longer.

I hadn't spoken aloud in months. Or was it years? I didn't know how long it had been since I had heard another voice.

I was cocooned in my silence.

The birds teased me overhead. They weren't tied to earth, and they didn't burn with hunger that could not be extinguished by death.

Sometimes they flew in pairs.

I felt life ebbing out of me by the moment as I stretched out on my rocks under Sun. Surely, soon there would be peace.

CHAPTER THIRTY-EIGHT

Intruders

I felt the presence of others shattering my silence. Intruders had entered my small, windy space; intruders with voices. I didn't want to hear human voices. I wanted bird voices. I wanted to speak in bird tongues. I wanted to cover my ears with my hands, but I no longer had the strength to move them.

Something amazingly fragrant was put in front of my traitorous mouth, arousing the thirst that I had thrust back. I bit. As the fluid spilled down my throat, I sat up. I grabbed for the source and growled, clutching the softness against my chest, feeling it fall to pieces in my hands, sucking until it was gone.

In despair, I realized I had polluted myself. Maybe Sun had been almost ready to receive me, and now my chance was ruined. I had felt a white light flowing over me before the intruders, and it dissipated after I drank.

Slowly, I came out of my blood-induced haze.

I opened my eyes and looked up. There were two of them staring down at me, their eyes glowing red. They looked familiar. The one crouched over me had a face I knew, one I had tried to push out of my memories. I closed my eyes; I refused to return to that world.

I felt arms slipping under me, lifting me. Funny, they felt warm. I remembered his arms as being cold and dead. I realized that he probably planned to move me away from my chosen spot, here at the end of the world.

I pushed away from him with a strength that surprised me, scrambling backwards on my hands until I was at the edge of a rock. I looked behind and saw the ocean's waves breaking below. Struggling to my feet, I balanced on the edge of the rock, watching the two demons approaching me. I leapt over them landing on the other side of my little promontory. The sea was below, and I paused before diving when I heard a familiar sound. One of the demons called to the other, "Mack." That word meant something to me once, but I tried to push it back.

I turned to see the demon had moved the rock covering my small cave and found my wings. He called the other to look at his discovery, and I swung back toward them with a snarl. They wouldn't be allowed to defile my wings with their touch. I had to defend them.

Instead of leaping into the ocean, I pounced.

CHAPTER THIRTY-NINE

Return

I leapt across the rock onto the back of the one who had dared defile my wings by touching them. I heard the first demon coming behind me, so I knew I didn't have much time. Though I aimed for his neck, my teeth sank into his shoulder, and I bit hard. His howl of pain was satisfying. The other came behind me and tried to pry apart my jaws to free his friend.

At the last second, I loosened my jaws and snapped onto the new one's hand. *Weren't expecting that, were you?* But I couldn't continue to fight two of them. I'd burnt through the small amount of strength given to me by the blood. I collapsed onto the rocks.

They grabbed me by my hands and feet, stretching me out and making it harder for me to reach them with my teeth. I felt them carrying me, but I kept my eyes closed, despairing at being taken away from my isolated spot where I was so close to the release of death.

We traveled a long time. Though I kept my eyes closed, I could feel the light of Sun shining down on us. Finally, we entered a closed space. I snapped my eyes open and looked around. My memories tried to tell me the space was a plane, but I pushed them back, refusing to submit to a world of human thought.

After a while, we left the tiny space, and they carried me somewhere else. I refused to look—I continued to fight the return to the human world I had been attempting to purge from my consciousness. Sometimes I keened from hunger, but I wouldn't eat what they put in front of me, however appetizing it smelled.

Eventually, we stopped moving and they released me. I opened my eyes.

We were in a dark place with cold walls. I shrank against them, feeling my way around the dim enclosure. The stone was too smooth to be a natural rock wall. My memories told me I was in a basement.

I shook my head to clear it. No human thoughts. They were weak.

No Sun shone above me in this place, only darkness. I needed to get out. Be free.

I fought, but they pushed food into me. They held my mouth open and poured something down my throat. My body drank thirstily, regaining strength. I started to fight again.

Eventually I broke free of their grip and assumed my pose. Right foot against left knee, both arms held above my head in a v, fingers pointed down.

I was certain that my feathers would come if I stood this way. Sometimes I could sense their prickle along my shoulders.

Would Sun find me here in this darkness?

CHAPTER FORTY

Time at an End

Being around these demons had taken a toll. I spent most of my time in my corner, prepared to strike, but I was losing the battle—they were pulling me back into a human world.

There were four of them. I forced myself not to think of them as individuals, but memories came back, triggered by the sound of their voices as they whispered.

The hair on one of these whisperers was brown. My hair was blonde, or it used to be. There was a cat somewhere with black hair. No, not hair. He had black fur.

I didn't want to listen to their voices. Yet I was bathed in them. Swirling sounds, surrounding me in waves of words. They were calling me back, back to a world where I was human, to where pain, fear and vulnerability ruled.

The one who never left, who ate in front of me and forced me to eat was the most persistent. I could feel him, calling to me with more than his voice.

Occasionally he pulled something over my body. My memories recognized it from the feel. Clothing. A dress. But those belong to the weak and vulnerable, a world where pain and fear rule all. I refused to go back there; I tore it off instantly.

I had only let him get close for one purpose—to fight. When he pulled the dress over my head, I could lean in and get a nice bite.

Only now he bit me back. I could feel him pumping something into me through his bite, massive amounts. It hurt, and I fought him, thrashing and biting. We had bitten one another so many times that I could feel his essence running through my body. I could sense his emotions sometimes if he managed to catch my eyes, locking me in place, pulling me back into his world.

The feelings were more insidious than the words they kept spewing at me. Eventually the words made sense, however resistant I was to them.

The first words that truly made sense to me were spoken by one of the infrequent visitors to my stony prison. He was one of the two demons who had brought me here. He had left though and only visited occasional- ly. I had resisted the others for so long that I had become immune to their voices. But this visitor's words broke through my consciousness.

"She's too far gone," he said. "And she's taking you with her, can't you see that? Let her go."

I wanted to scream, "Let her go!" at them, but I wouldn't let them know I heard and understood.

Eventually I broke free and assumed my pose. Right foot against left knee, arms in a v above my head, fingers pointed down. Waiting for the feathers to erupt from my arms, while the familiar stranger shook his head and left.

CHAPTER FORTY-ONE

The Old One

I sensed a different feeling in the room. A sense of nervous anticipation.

A light shone from the top of the room, high above the floor as a door opened. I saw a glimpse of a profile at the top of the stairs, a new visitor, someone I hadn't seen before. Broad shoulders, black hair to his shoulder blades. Even from where I stood in my corner, I could feel his age and his power. This new being was stronger than the others.

I hissed as I backed into my corner, going into my pose, hands above me, one leg bent upwards, prepared to strike.

He walked down the stairs, waved the others away, and stood in front of me.

Feeling threatened I dropped from my pose and backed along the wall, trying to get away from him.

He followed me and started talking. I ducked my head, closing my eyes and pushing away his words, batting at them with my hands. Words, like feelings, were dangerous in their ability to bind and pull me back into their world.

He looked behind me, and for some reason I sensed a threat to the brown-maned one, the one who fed me even if against my will. I was surprised to find myself stepping in front of him protectively, hissing at the stranger in front of us.

There was a long pause, and I felt arms slip around my waist as the one I was protecting whispered words in my ear. I shook my head to keep the words from entering my brain, but I felt a reassuring tone, and I relaxed.

The newcomer was still standing in front of us, regarding us steadily chin in one hand. He stood that way for a while as I stared at him, my hands touching the arms of the one behind me. Suddenly the old one grabbed me and sank his teeth into my neck. Hard. I struggled against him, but the other pinned my hands at my waist and held me still.

Waves of something flowed over me and through me, reaching deep inside.

I howled and screamed as words and memories flowed back into me, everything I had pushed away.

Images of Mama. Mama looking down at me while I reached up for her face. Of walking. Of eating. Blueberries. Bike riding. School. Pictures flashed by in my head—too fast—and I let go of the old one as I tried to bat them away until finally blackness overwhelmed me.

CHAPTER FORTY-TWO

Waking Up

I sank into blackness, sweet nothingness. I surrendered to it, willing the hunger and yearnings to go away forever.

Yet even as I was letting go, the others wouldn't leave me alone. I felt someone calling me. I came back to make them stop, putting a hand to my throbbing neck, sitting up and looking around.

Faces. I recognized them. Mr. Amalfi. He was worthy of a low hiss. His face was smiling, but his expression wavered as I hissed. Then another face, the one who had held me. Mack.

In the past he had stolen me from my world, but he had been with me ever since. A presence. Now, he felt like an extension of myself. I looked at his hand on my waist and then glanced down and immediately covered myself.

I was naked. Where were my clothes?

Mack handed me something. "Here."

It was a dress. I quickly shredded while pulling it over my head.

"Let me help," he said.

I shook my head, clearing it, as his voice was confusing me.

He wrapped me in a blanket then took off his shirt.

I stood still while Mack pulled the shirt over me then looked up at the imposing figure in front of us. Dark hair, deep thoughtful eyes.

This newcomer had bit me. When he spoke, his voice came out rich and deep, full of authority but also compassion and curiosity.

"You know me, don't you, little one?"

"Moltadano," I croaked out, my voice unexpectedly raspy. He watched me for a few seconds, his eyes looking deep into me, cool yet sympathetic.

"What does my name mean to you?" he asked, his voice low and sweet, seeming to pull answers from me.

"You kill vampires," I said.

A brief smile ghosted across his face. "Only those who need or want it," he said calmly. "I would have thought that was what you wanted."

Mack snarled but went silent when Moltadano gave him a sharp look.

When they looked at one another, their attention was momentarily diverted from me. That's what I was waiting for, and I made my move, running up the stairs. I felt them turn and reach for me, but I was already out of their grasp.

I smashed through the door at the top of the stairs and ran into a vampire, a tall one, who grabbed me and flipped me back onto the ground, pinning me to the floor.

"Hey, hey, settle down," he said. He was familiar, and I remembered him as having been terrifying in the past. I chomped on one of the arms holding me, kicking and punching at him at the same time.

I heard Mack and the others come up behind me.

"She's never tried to come up the stairs before," the vampire holding me said, tugging at my jaw to detach my teeth from his arm. "That's quite a bite. C'mon, let go!"

I shook my head and tore at his arm a little more before finally releasing it.

"She's human again, or rather, she no longer thinks she's a bird," Mack said, reaching for me.

The other man grunted and rubbed at his arm before pulling it to his mouth to lick the wound.

I looked around with new eyes. Memories were returning, all the things I had pushed back. I felt a new presence inside though. In addition to the human girl Christa there was this new being, a bird-girl, strengthened by years of running and isolation, one who was powerful and strong. I shifted my shoulders, letting these selves adjust to their surroundings.

I stared at the one of the vampires in front of me. Mr. Amalfi was tall, elegantly dressed. He was the art dealer I met by the fountain in Italy and sat next to on the airplane to New York. Looking around the room, I saw it was elegantly furnished, so we were probably in his house. It was decorated with antiques, and I was currently making holes in a beautiful oriental rug. There were things hanging on the wall that weren't making sense to me. When I focused on their shapes, I recognized paintings. With my new eyesight initially I could only see bits of paint placed on canvas, but they eventually resolved into scenes. Street scenes of foreign places suspended from the walls in heavy, gilded frames.

The room's large windows were hung with heavy drapes made of deep blue, with braided gold cords to hold them in place. If those drapes were open what framed scenes would they display? A city street? An ocean?

This had been above me all those months? I had been in a stone basement room beneath such luxury? Glancing at the shredded rug beneath me I realized they probably just wanted to keep these precious items upstairs safe.

Looking at one of the men, I remembered. He had come to the house, and Lillian had told me his name. Ted, that was it. Lillian?

A sudden pang went through me as the name Lillian flitted across my mind.

I turned back to the man, Mack. "Lillian?" I asked.

"Over here, doll," a soft voice said.

I turned. I saw a slender woman with mouse brown hair. She was wearing a blue print dress, sitting in a rocking chair by a window. It was Lillian, and she was okay. I was glad.

In front of me was the brown-maned one. Mack. Mr. Samuels. I felt a growl coming out which I tried to restrain. I crouched and out of the corner of my eye saw a few of the others tense, but they were stilled by a gesture from Moltadano. He stood, imperious, watching me carefully, rubbing his chin with his hand.

Moltadano had the power I sensed. It felt good to know who had the power in this group. Who I had to kill, if necessary, to get what I needed. But I had the feeling I wouldn't have to kill Moltadano. He had done what he came to do.

I cut my eyes from Moltadano and focused my attention on Mack. Pulling back slightly to get a better spring, I pounced.

Mack let me leap on top of him. Instead of fighting he merely put his hand in front of his face. Once I had

him down, I looked at him more closely. He was handsome with a nice build. Lean and long-waisted, with
muscles showing under his shirt. Right now he had one
of his hands on my shoulder to prevent my teeth from
easily reaching his neck.

As he lay on the floor, I thought how pretty his hair
looked fanned out around his head. I reached out to
touch it and felt him relax.

He looked like a lion. I turned my head to view him
from a different angle. Most definitely a lion.

I pulled back and kneaded his chest a little. He
purred.

He would make a nice lion. I was going to keep him
as my pet.

I smiled down at him, and his rumbling purr
stopped. He stiffened and went on guard. I narrowed my
eyes. He knew I was a threat.

Good.

Behind me, I heard Moltadano laugh. "You wanted
her, and you got her."

I kneaded Mack's chest again, beginning the long
work of making this creature my lion pet.

ABOUT THE AUTHOR

Katy Mann grew up in the Midwest and currently lives
in California.

Visit her at www.KatyMann.com.